The Brown Code

A NOVEL

The Brown Code

By Jack Dunn

Copyright © 2014 by Jack Dunn
All rights reserved.

ISBN: 1500723282
ISBN 13: 9781500723286

No part of this book may be used or reproduced without written permission except in the case of brief quotations. This is a work of historical fiction and individual characters portrayed in it are fictional. Any resemblance to actual persons is entirely coincidental.

DEDICATION

A story...speaks for itself.

AUTHOR'S NOTE

Christianity and Faith in general throughout the world *is* **a target** of this conspiracy!

ACKNOWLEDGMENTS

The **common information, original creations**, the **sequence of events and scenes** and **the characters specific order of appearances** and **their interactions** were invaluable to me in producing this work.

Jack Dunn
July, 2014

Jack Dunn has written ten books and two movie screenplays. A writer has gained international fame and wealth, but only with the favorable treatment of a federal judge.

The Brown Code

The Vatican pontifical prelature known as Opus Dei is an ultraconservative, powerful Catholic sect that built an intricate worldwide financial network around the world. There are reports of members who were *troubled souls* and the Catholic Church's *Devil's Advocates* were investigating the brainwashing, women trafficking and corporeal mortification said to be practiced in the Opus Dei organization. Some men like the illustrious Leonardo Da Vinci were former Masonic grandmasters of a Knight's brotherhood with lineages to a European secret society of warrior monks and Knights that was founded in Jerusalem in the 11th Century, just before to the First Crusade.

The Paris Enquirer June 14, 1996

Pope John Paul I, who died in 1978, was the victim of a plot by the P2 Masonic Lodge. It's alleged that the secret society murdered John Paul I when it found out that he was going to expose the American Archbishop Paul Marcincus as President of the Vatican Bank. The Bank has been implicated in shady financial dealings with the Opus Dei and the Masonic Lodge.

Boston Weekly News June 18, 1996

This was a plot that revolved around a powerful, ruthless and covert Masonic Lodge having links directly to the Vatican.

PROLOGUE

LONDON —

A 60-year old Mason man is murdered because he knows a secret about a Catholic Church brotherhood

Renowned financier Leonardo Roberto Calvi stumbled through a high structure in the museum's Grand Hall. He grabbed for a case he dropped on the floor that had information in it linking him to a $790 million bank fraud. Grasping the painting hanging next to him on a wall the sixty-one year old man tore the canvas off from its binding as he fell to the floor beneath it. Calvi felt like he was almost out of time and could hardly catch his breath.

Just as he thought this a heavy steel door opened nearby that locked off the section he was in from the other galleries of the museum. The floor shook for a second and then an alarm could be heard ringing throughout the building.

The banker lay silent for a moment thinking that he should have committed suicide and not still be alive. Hearing noises he scampered into a corner looking for someplace to hide.

The voice that spoke to him was forceful, "Don't move."

Still on the floor the old man looked up panicked to see what he had feared for weeks now. They had finally found him.

Only ten feet away near the steel door a man's enormous outline appeared. He was the killer sent to find Calvi by a brotherhood because he knew a secret about the Catholic Church.

The pale-faced attacker had a gun in his hand and it was aimed at the frightened man on the floor. "You've been running long enough.

"I told you," the old man stammered, "I don't know what you're talking about. I deny everything."

"You possess something that is not yours," the attacker shouted out forcefully. "Tell me where it's hidden or I'll kill you."

Calvi gasped for air trying to breathe. "I'll tell you what you want to know."

"The other three bankers said the same thing," the attacker said once Calvi finished talking. "It's common amongst you all."

A loud bang echoed through the walls of the museum. The bullet the attacker fired hit Calvi in the pit of his stomach.

Calvi crawled along the floor bleeding and in pain. He murmured out softly, "I have passed on the secret.

They'll never get it. The mission we've guarded for generations is safe."

The attacker grabbed Calvi by his coat and dragged him to a doorway with an overhang. Throwing a rope up and over a beam he tied it off and placed a noose around Calvi's neck. Pulling hard at the rope he slowly lifted the banker into the air until his feet were off the ground. "You're going to join your three dead brethren."

"There's only one person on earth who knows the secret," Calvi uttered defiantly as he felt the rope tighten, beginning to strangle him to death. His neck bones were popping out where they had been snapped, and his head was twisted completely around, looking backwards.

"Well I guess I'm going to have to find the person who knows this elusive secret," the attacker said gleefully watching Calvi take his last breaths. "It's what the *Pope's Secretary hired me to do.*"

ONE

April, 1996
April in New England

The Awful Dream (Nightmare)

Tucked away in the mountains of Vermont, Hope House provided its guests with temporary separation from the toils of the world. However, it was anything but a peaceful place. The old mental hospital had become a rehabilitation facility, a place where one could detoxify one's body from drugs and alcohol, but not without a great deal of torment and suffering.

For Sophie Turrell on this unusually *cold* spring day, the *beauty of the grounds*, the grace of the old grey stone buildings, and the majestic sweep of the Green Mountains, softened by the late afternoon light, *contrasted sharply with* the pain of her withdrawal symptoms. In another frame of mind, the rural setting might inspire inner peace and *tranquility but now it only sharpened her feelings of hopelessness and anguish.*

She was lovely. Thirty-five years old, standing feet-eleven-inches tall, with blonde hair, classic features, and deep-set *blue eyes*, she had the elegant demeanor of *upper-class privilege*, the kind that causes both men and women *to stare* and envision themselves at her side. *But her eyes were dull now and her hair listless, her face was grey, her body weak.* A deep tremor shook her and she turned away from the window, watching the blue curtain drift back across the small squares of cold glass.

Coming here had not been her idea, but she couldn't remember whose it was, and now she was too sick to leave. *Lying on the stiff white sheets of the narrow bed,* she pondered the question until a soothing veil of *sleep* dropped softly over her.

Then the *awful dream* began again. She is on the *high bridge*, *alone* and afraid. It is snowing heavily and winds blow relentlessly. She *struggles* to cross the rickety foot-bridge, *hanging onto* slender frozen ropes, her hands torn and bleeding. A battered sign reads, *Bridge of Dread.* Seeing it, her strength and nerve fail. *Darkness engulfs her*; she *can see neither the beginning nor the end*, yet knows she *is halfway across* or nearly so, and *must reach* the other side. She crawls and scratches blindly along the worn boards, slipping on mounds of packed snow and ice, and then she *hears the voices*—the deep, *mocking laughter* of those who had fallen off—rising up from the abyss. She *senses a presence* creeping up from behind and *peers back* into the darkness. Dragging itself along, a *hideous gorgon* is approaching her. A *wave of panic* washes over her and she charges forward, only to slip uncontrollably. As she does, another presence flies free above her, soaring effortlessly into the terrifying winds, and it whispers as it passes over her. It is a *magical* winged icon. She manages to make some headway and is *reaching out* when a *frightening shriek pierces the air* of the night. The icon has found its mark! But when she *turns to look*, the gorgon is still alive, still stalking her.

Sophie *awoke, gasping, drenched with sweat*. She wiped the wetness on her face with the sleeve of her nightgown and shakily *switched on the lamp next to her bed*. The room was *empty*. She *tried to focus* on a seascape hanging lopsided on the wall opposite her, but as soon as she moved, her head began to pound and *nausea* forced her back down. Making a tremendous effort, she steadied herself and sat up. Blood rushed to her head but she was determined to remain upright. Slowly, she freed herself from the bedding twisted around her feet and let the blanket slide to the floor.

Dr. Maximilian Maxwell was listening in the hallway outside. He had been called by the floor nurse when the screaming began. Knocking gently on her half-opened door, he entered and found his patient huddled on the floor near the bed. Slowly, he walked over to her. The room reeked of sweat and vomit.

"Sophie? It's Dr. Maximilian, *the Director*. *I'm waking you up*." He raised her chin and tried to find a spark in her eyes. "You've had a rather rough time of it."

Sophie dropped her head and the deep, wracking sobs began.

The counselor helped her onto the bed and put his arm around her until her sobbing became a *howl of anguish* and then subsided. Gently, he pushed the wet hair from her eyes, then pulled up an armchair in the bed and sat down in it.

"How do you feel?" he asked, feeling slightly foolish for the triteness of the question.

"Like I'm in hell," she gasped.

He looked down at the wet sheets and the vivid pink scar circling her upper thigh.

"You had *the dream again?*" he asked. "*It's a reoccurring nightmare.*"

"I don't remember much except feeling sick and screaming. Was I yelling? What was I screaming about?" She looked blankly at him.

"I'm not sure," he said. Not wanting to discuss the dream yet, he went on. "But I'd like you to attend a group session. Get yourself cleaned up and come down to the meeting room. I think you're ready for it and you need it. It's the last door down the hall on the left. We start in an hour."

"Who's we?"

"Me and several other patients. Don't worry. I'll take it slow."

He sensed her apprehension and took her *trembling hands* into his. "Sophie, it's time to take the next step."

She looked into his face, desperately *wanting to trust him, but deeply afraid.* "I don't know. I'm not sure I can," she said, looking away from him, fearing everything.

"All I'm asking you to do is to show up. Nothing more," he tried to reassure her. "*I want you to come there.*"

Momentarily, Sophie quieted herself. "All right. I'll come."

"Good," said Maximilian. He gave her a hug and left the room, closing the door quietly behind him.

Sophie tried to stand but *the dizziness* made it difficult, almost impossible. Holding onto the bed, then the dresser, the wall, and finally the bathroom door, she made it into the bathroom. After a long hot shower she managed to dress herself. Her black slacks and sweater hung loosely on her now and when *she looked in the mirror*, the *haggard face she saw there was almost unknown to her*. She *felt physically light and emotionally heavy.*

"What the hell am I doing here?" she asked *the specter*, *a ghost* looking back at her. "*I'm the only one who knows why the Mason man was murdered.*"

TWO

Sunday, January 5, 1964

'The Teacher' and the Sacred Treasure — the relic that will bring enormous power

It all began with a piece of cloth.
A small, thin man carried with him *the sacred trea-*
The cloth was so carefully hidden that even those traveling with him did not know of it, as they made their pilgrimage into the hills of Galilee to the Church of the Multiplication in the village of Tabgha.

The bearded, forty-seven-year-old parish priest there had spent days preparing for the pope's arrival. His church had been scrubbed clean and its tarnished metals polished bright by two old women from the village. Fresh flowers decorated the altar and the newly washed stained glass windows glowed in the morning's sunlight. Everything was made ready to receive the blessed Holy Father.

The Brown Code

Father Leigh Rovarik was in the sanctuary removing his vestments when the long white limousine arrived. Trying to prepare himself, he wondered once more why he had been chosen to guard *the artifact*. Not really having the answer, he knew only that he would accept it humbly and guard it forever with his life.

Two plainclothes papal gendarmes opened the car door for the pope, who stepped heavily and a bit unhappily into the bright, dry, day.

Father Rovarik, still in his white cassock, walked out to greet him. His welcoming smile warmed the slightly built aging pontiff upon whose shoulder was slung a black leather satchel.

"Papa, how honored and happy I am to see you." Rovarik knelt and kissed *the ring* of Peter. "Come, come and refresh yourself." Rovarik gestured to the modest rectory next to the church.

"Thank you, Leigh. But first, won't you show me your beautiful church?" replied Paul.

The two sandaled men turned to climb the few steps up to the open front doors and then walked through the church talking in low voices. In the sacristy, alone with Father Rovarik, Paul placed a hand on the younger man's shoulder.

"My old friend," he said, "I know of no one else who possesses the love and courage equal to this enormous task. I will pray for your safety every day of my life."

The Holy Father opened his bag, removed a tissue-wrapped article and held it out to him. Rovarik bowed his head and silently took the cloth from the pontiff's hands.

It was one hour later when the men from Rome left to continue their epic journey through the holy lands of Israel. Only the village priest and the pope knew that something of enormous significance had just occurred.

It had been Pope Paul VI's namesake, the *apostle Paul*, who was the first steward of the *precious object*. He had brought it before the *Council of Jerusalem in 49 A.D.,* where he cautioned the other apostles that Christianity must never be allowed to become a closed, possessive system, and preached that the gifts and the spiritual thoughts imparted to them by Christ were for the benefit of all the peoples of the world without restrictions or exclusions.

"Beware of those who will manipulate the beliefs of *The Teacher*," he had warned. "They will one day try to seize the reins of power and desecrate the ageless truths of the master, Jesus Christ." Even the wisdom of the Savior could be turned into tools for profit, he told them, and the words of the Lord could be misconstrued or misinterpreted by those trying to do so.

Saint Paul had envisioned a time when the meek would indeed inherit the earth and prophesied a second coming of the Messiah, when all that they had witnessed would be seen again. "Someday," he said, "all the cultures of the world will understand these eternal truths and the religion we are founding will be the moving force unifying all the people, transcending the rites, rituals, and belief systems of all religions.

Finally, he had repeated what *Jesus* had told him when He had entrusted him with *the sacred object*: "The power is in the revelations I have given to you.

Those who desecrate my teachings will feel the wrath of God."

The pope's limousine traveled only a few miles from the church before it was halted by a sudden swirling dust storm. The pope left the car and began threading his way down a rocky path that cut between a stand of tall pines and scattered eucalyptus trees to a lake. At the edge of the lake stood a carved stone statue, the Sanctuary of the Primacy of Peter. Two thousand years ago, the resurrected Jesus Christ had faced Saint Peter in this exact spot and told him to "Feed my lambs."

Now the 262nd successor to the first shepherd fell to his knees and prayed that *'the relic'* he had just passed on would someday bring the churches of the world together to tend to the Lord's flock. Suspecting the imminent fate, however, of his beloved Catholic Church, his tears of sorrow fell onto the same holy ground where Jesus had walked.

THREE

**Rome, Italy
May 17, 1992**

*A 1990's Conclave in Rome is controlled by
The Pope's Secretary*

Pope John Paul II, resplendent in white and gold Vestments, was sweating profusely as he stood before the hastily constructed altar in St. Peter's Square. Nevertheless, he ignored the sweltering heat and dutifully conferred the rites of beatification upon Josemaria Escriva de Balaguer.

Monsignor Escriva had founded an ultraconservative religious movement, the Opus Dei, at a small church in Spain in 1928. Since then, the sect had spread its teachings around the world. Demanding absolute loyalty to the authority of the Opus Dei and the pope, Escriva had quietly laid the groundwork not only for his own religious organization, but for an intricate worldwide financial empire exercising considerable influence on the church. Working inside the Vatican, he had bent and molded its primary offices to accumulate enormous power for himself and the Opus Dei.

It was perhaps because of this influence that the beatification was taking place a mere seventeen years after his death. The event marked some of the greatest changes in procedure ever to take place in Western religious history. More than a few church members had protested Escriva's candidacy, pointing out that he had not been adequately investigated by the *Devil's Advocates*, church elders appointed to prove or disprove a life of heroic virtue of any candidate chosen for sainthood. Studying Escriva's writings and practices and investigating the claims of miracles performed by him should have taken decades, even centuries. There had been reports that Escriva had openly sympathized with Adolph Hitler, perhaps finding a brother in the quest for world domination or a fellow troubled soul with a similar family history of abuse and emotional control.

Even so, he was being beatified on this humid day in St. Peter's Square with over 200,000 faithful souls bearing witness to the historic event. The ceremony was the centerpiece of a *Conclave* of Opus Dei officials to set the organization's future agenda and to plan tactics to strengthen its financial position in the church. Once the sacred rites had been performed, the pope ordered the remains of Monsignor Scoria's casket to be brought from a small church on Bruno Buozzi, where they had been since his death, and moved to the sacred Vatican crypts.

The plain wooden coffin was transported the following day. To prepare the bones for the pope's ritual blessing, it was opened by a group of Opus Dei priests. Immediately, they saw that something was wrong inside. Escriva was supposed to have been covered with a sacred cloth, brought to him many years ago by a mystical Gypsy woman.

The holy relic added credibility to the rightness of his mission and the holiness of his life. But the cloth that lay over his corpse was decomposing. Seeing this, the priests sent for Manuel Zagranski, *the chief secretary to the pope*, who had personally seen *the relic* on several occasions. Being the first person ever to hold both positions he had knowledge no one else had about the Catholic Church's secret activities. Without a doubt, he attested, the disintegrating piece of material draped over Escriva's body was a fake.

Quiet plans that had taken nearly four decades to piece together had to be quickly changed and the fear that the real cloth might be lost forever to them drove the Opus Dei leaders into a panic.

Silas Willoughby was one of the spectators in Vatican City on the day of the contested beatification. He had flown in from a coastal town in Maine a few days earlier upon *special invitation from Archbishop Zagranski.*

Silas was a mercenary. He had been trained for the work by his father, a former military man skilled in special operations. As soon as he had turned 18, Silas had joined the Marines and gained valuable experience during several tours of duty in Cambodia and

Lebanon. Now his *services were available* to anyone with enough money to employ him. The officials of the Opus Dei knew him to be well versed in covert operations and had chosen him to head up their new secret military order. Four years later it would be Silas who would be sent to find the ancient cloth that was supposed to be covering Escriva's body.

FOUR

Logan International Airport
June 4, 1996

> *Robert is called by the Director*
> *and goes to the Institute*
>
> *The woman who knows the secret is there*
>
> *The Director talks to Robert about Sophie*

Two planes, one from Paris and one from London, landed at Logan International Airport in Boston within an hour of each other. Two men, one from each plane, met in the baggage claim area and then, talking quietly, walked to one of the car rental counters. Jamie Cole was the taller of the two—six foot three with features too worn for his 39 years. He was stocky, almost fat, and his body showed signs of neglect and overeating. His short reddish-brown hair was messy, his grey

Brooks Brothers suit wrinkled, and his demeanor was most unfriendly.

His friend of 20 years, Robert Hathaway, had a *commanding appearance*. Though considerably shorter and no younger than Jamie, he was a vital, attractive man with dark hair and *intense blue eyes*. His *dress was casual — jeans,* sneakers, and a leather jacket—but the jeans were tailored and pressed, the sneakers new and white, and the leather of his jacket was a soft suede. As always, he had an *engaging smile on his face, the kind women love*.

Jamie found a cigarette machine while Robert took care of the rental car arrangements. The middle-aged agent behind the counter sighed, fluffed her hair and lingered over her directions to the parking lot where they would find their car. She couldn't help but flirt with Robert, although he gave her no encouragement.

Outside, Robert got into the car on the driver's side, knowing how much Jamie hated to drive, especially in large cities where speeding and traffic were the norm. He noticed the car phone hooked up on the console. No phone had been requested. Robert pointed to it and put his fingers to his lips. Jamie grunted with annoyance as he fastened his seat belt.

Twenty minutes later, after a brief stop to disconnect the phone wires, they were traveling west toward Vermont. Still concerned that there might be a bug in the car, they were careful about what they said.

"Why do you think the *Director* positioned just the two of us *here at Logan*," Robert asked, "There are other airports closer to the action."

"Just convenient," Jamie answered, "I'm still trying to figure out why he put me on an experimental space shuttle airplane and landed it here. Hell I thought it wasn't going to stop until we got to Fenway Park."

"Sophie went to school in Switzerland," Robert said, thinking about it.

"Somewhere around Geneva," Jamie added.

"You look tired, Jamie!"

"Things at the center are hectic, old buddy. Life seems much more complicated than when we were younger."

"How's the new venture going?"

"Slowly, and it's pretty frustrating. We've been getting a lot of grief from the committee about expenditures and budgets and I feel like we're spending more time finding ways to hold onto the funding than doing research and development. They're idiots!" Jamie muttered as he sipped black coffee from a Styrofoam cup.

"Money is money! They're paid to do what they do, which is watch the cash registers. They could care less about anything else. You know that."

"It doesn't make things go better or progress faster if they badger us for results before we're ready. These things take time. I don't have to tell you that."

"How far are you from finishing?"

"A year, unless we hit another snag."

Robert looked at his old friend and smiled. "I'll see if I can get them to lay off when I get back. I'll talk to a few of the investors."

"Tell them that if they don't, they might be looking for another department head. I've had about enough of their bullshit."

"Let's not start this all over again. If you blow your stack again, you'll be in a lot of trouble. It won't be as easy to reposition you now as it was last time. I had to chase you down in Amsterdam and I can't do that again."

"Ahh, Amsterdam... nasty Amsterdam... shit, did we have a good time there or what!" Jamie laughed.

"Yeah. Remember the night Sophie and I found you in the red light district and ended up floating around on a gondola with you and that Australian bimbo from the Old Sailor Hotel?"

"Hey, it's easy to get lost in the canals, Robert," Jamie grinned.

"You stole the goddamn boat and fell in the drink! Jesus, I thought you drowned. You should have seen the expression on Sophie's face when you climbed back into the boat screaming about sharks."

The two laughed and relaxed for a moment, remembering the closeness they had shared. They reminisced about less stressful times, when they *were younger*, optimistic, and still getting to know each other.

Two hours later they were sitting in the small office of Dr. Maximilian Maxwell in Brattleboro. He offered them coffee, which Jamie accepted and Robert declined. Maximilian closed the blinds behind his desk against the afternoon sun. They talked briefly and vaguely about Sophie. Maximilian was guarded about his concerns.

"When she arrived here, she was immobilized physically and mentally from alcohol and drug abuse. In addition to her obvious dependencies, she is suffering from paranoia. She believes *someone is after her* and will find and kill her."

Robert was listening intently. "How did she get here in the first place?" he asked quietly.

"That's a good question. I returned to the clinic after a holiday. She had been admitted involuntarily over the weekend." He opened Sophie's file. "There were some ID cards, but there are many questions concerning her real identity and there is no record of who brought her in."

He looked closely at the two men and decided to go on. "The person who brought her left a telephone number in New York, but it is not a working number and that person's name isn't in the telephone directory. He apparently didn't want to get involved. We've been trying to find anyone who can help identify her. We weren't even sure that Sophie Turrell is her real name. We called the local authorities and they said they would run a check on her and get back to us." He paused again. Jamie glanced over at Robert, who blinked and crossed his legs.

"Like I said, she was admitted with very little identification on her and only a few personal belongings. Actually, all she had were the clothes on her back and a little money."

"Don't worry about the costs. I'll take care of everything," Robert dismissed the fee issue. "How did you get my name and number?" he wondered.

"*I called you*, Mr. Hathaway, because she repeated your name and telephone number frequently during her delirium. I wrote it down, although it was a reach. I took a chance and *got in touch with you because she's in a great deal of trouble* and needs a lot of help."

Maximilian sat back in his chair and looked across his desk at Robert and Silas, waiting for a response, whether it was an expression of concern or information about Sophie. Anything. But the men were strangely reticent.

Finally, Jamie spoke up. "Did she mention any other names?"

"Well, she has referred to many persons, but by description rather than name. Mr. Hathaway was the only person she named. *She seems to be good with numbers*. Parts of her ramblings were filled with numbers. Like I said, that's how I got your phone number. I questioned her about you, but she doesn't tell us much about her relationships. I suspect that you are more than just a friend because of some of the things she said about you, even though she's been mostly incoherent. I have gotten very little direct information from her. She is lucid now but has not communicated consistently."

"No one has called asking about her?" Robert asked.

"No, no one. Why do you ask?"

"Then, to your knowledge, we are the only ones who know she is here?" Robert leaned forward with a very direct look into Maximilian's eyes. The doctor pulled back as strong suspicions about the men began to emerge. Who were they? Why weren't they more concerned about Sophie's state of mind? Robert sensed his distrust and countered it immediately.

"This is all such a shock. The whole thing is just so strange. I had no idea Sophie was in so much trouble. We've been friends for years..." Robert's voice trailed off as he sat back in his chair, shaking his head. "We'll help her in any way we can."

Maximilian had been looking for this kind of statement and felt somewhat calmer. But he chose his next words carefully. "She's still chemically dependent and may be on the verge of a complete breakdown. She feels alone and abandoned."

Robert shook his head again and sighed. "How long do you plan on keeping her here, Dr. Maxwell?" "As long as it takes to help her get well or until she decides she's had enough of us. She's not under any court order to stay and is free to leave on her own volition at any time."

Robert sighed again, cleared his throat, and sat back.

"Can we visit with her?" Jamie asked.

"Yes, but I want to caution you to be careful about what you say. She's still under a lot of pressure."

"We understand. We'll be gentle," Robert answered.

"If you would be kind enough to wait out in the hall, I'll bring her to the conference room where you can talk without being disturbed."

"Thank you, doctor," Jamie said as he grasped Maximilian's hand clumsily once they walked out of the office.

The three friends huddled together in the dimly lit conference room, hugging each other tightly. They said nothing for several minutes. Tears expressed their love for one another and the torment they all felt for the situation. Robert was the first to break the embrace and the silence.

"Why didn't you call me when you knew what was happening to you?" he asked gently. Sophie didn't answer; her quiet sobbing prevented her from speaking. Jamie held her close, his large arm circling her bony shoulder, his thick hand awkwardly stroking her cheek. He dabbed at his own damp face with his coat sleeve.

Robert took one of her hands and cradled it in both of his. "How did you get in so deep?" he asked. "You should have called me, honey."

Sophie looked into his face, hoping to find the love they had once shared. "I'm tired, Robert. I'm tired. I don't have the strength to go through with it. I've gone too far. I've messed up. I... I've failed totally." She started to cry again.

"Don't worry about it, don't worry about anything." He took her face in his hands. "Just get yourself better. You won't have to handle it much longer. It's almost over. Tell us what happened and let us deal with it. *Then you'll be free of them forever.*"

"No, I can't, Robert, I can't."

Robert took her into his arms and tried to comfort her. "Listen, it's going to be all right. I'll talk to them. I'll explain."

Sophie became frantic. "No. No. It's too horrible. It's killing me. They're killing me." Her voice rose to a scream. She broke away from Robert. "Why did you leave me when I needed you?" She gave up and crumpled on the floor, crying deeply.

Jamie stood up. He was becoming very disturbed by the intensity of Sophie's distress. He wanted to leave and gestured to Robert for a word with him privately. "Let's go. She needs their help and some time to get better," he whispered, fingering his collar, genuinely concerned but uncomfortable, "and she's right. It's much more involved now."

"Shut up, Jamie. This is between Sophie and me. Wait by the door." Jamie threw his head back, walked over to the door, and leaned against the wall. He tried in vain to press out the wrinkles in his grey jacket with his hands.

Robert returned to Sophie and lowered himself onto the floor. "I'm so sorry, Sophie. I had no idea things were so bad." He waited a moment and then held his hand out to her again. She looked at it and then into his eyes, searching for his heart.

Robert left his hand open for her. "I'll take care of you," he said. He spoke very quietly. "I'll never leave you again." Sophie hesitated. "Never," he reassured her. Slowly she put her hand in his and he drew her to him. She relaxed in his arms and closed her eyes. His voice and touch quieted her. "I'll get you out of this. All I want is for you to be all right." He continued speaking softly and gently stroked her hair.

When they left, Sophie was drained. She returned to her room, lay down, and fell into a long, deep, dreamless sleep.

Robert and Jamie checked into the Maple Leaf Motel on Route 5. While Jamie showered, Robert sat in an uncomfortable chair on the balcony outside. The clear Vermont sky was full of twinkling stars. He thought that under the right circumstances, it would be nice to be here with Sophie.

Jamie ordered a bourbon and soda before a late dinner and Robert had scotch, neat. Jamie reiterated his concerns that Sophie was in critical need of treatment. Robert agreed but argued persuasively that she'd be much safer somewhere else. He reminded Jamie that she had been registered in her real name. "Once the police inquiry hits the network they'll know where to look. It's only a matter of time before they find her here," he said. Jamie reluctantly agreed and they decided to get Sophie out of the hospital as soon as possible.

The next morning they arrived at the Director's office as he was about to start his rounds. "Well," said. Maximilian, "Come in." He motioned for them to sit. "I understand you had quite a session with Sophie yesterday," he said, not altogether approving. "She is apparently still a bit shaken up."

Jamie looked chastened. "I think she needs some attention."

Maximilian concurred, nodding his head. "It could take months."

"Yeah," Jamie answered looking to Robert, who was spinning his sunglasses in his lap.

"Is there any previous history of drug abuse?" Maximilian couldn't help but feel that the men would be willing to share some information now that they had seen Sophie's condition.

"No," Robert said, looking up. "This is not the Sophie we know."

"Is she really running from someone? Afraid of someone?"

"Yes," Robert said simply.

Maximilian was alarmed that she could be in danger. "I sense that you're both familiar with whoever that someone might be. What do you know about this woman's predicament? Who is after her?"

Robert spoke calmly and plainly. "It's quite involved. There's a lot more going on with Sophie than the obvious."

"There always is. I've been impressed at her insight into her state of mind. She seems quite knowledgeable about many things. Her delusions, though, are the real issues in her treatment now."

Jamie looked at Robert, wondering how much he would say. Robert maintained his calm demeanor. He was relaxed but alert. "Sophie understands very well what's at the bottom of these problems. She is, as you say, highly intelligent. Unfortunately, this is not a remedy, as you know. And her paranoia is not psychotic nor is it about addiction."

"I agree, Mr. Hathaway!" Maximilian was eager to continue this promising conversation. "But the better I understand her situation the better I can help her. I need tools to help her rebuild the house," Maximilian said, trying to draw him out.

"Sophie has the tools, Dr. Maxwell, and her house is not the problem. It's a question of whether or not she can use them."

"Yes, I gather she's had some counseling before. But I'm asking you, her friends, to please give me some information that will help me move her toward recovery," Maximilian allowed some of his exasperation to show. They were as difficult to draw out as the woman was.

"Sophie is a very bright woman," Robert said. "She has a doctorate in economics and has been involved in several *research projects* and businesses. Of course, as you know, highly intelligent people are often the most difficult patients to work with."

The therapist sat back, thinking about Sophie's ranting about suicide and the many conversations he'd had with her. "Where has she worked?"

"*In London mostly*," Jamie answered, "at a number of universities and a few *private institutes*. Most recently she was positioned at the Shelley Institute in Chelsea."

"What kind of work was she doing there?" Maximilian thought there was a great deal missing from this description of his patient.

"*Just research*," Robert repeated.

"What kind of research?" Maximilian pressed. "It's important that I know."

"It was *a highly confidential project*, Dr. Maxwell. Let's leave it alone for now, shall we." Robert would not budge.

"Fine, but tell me, how does someone involved in a research program at a *private institute in London* find herself in a care facility in the Green Mountains of Vermont?

"Why wasn't she treated in London?"

"She took some matters into her own hands, Dr. Maxwell, and left the country in a hurry."

The answer did not satisfy Maximilian. "Really," he said, looking skeptically at Robert. "You aren't telling me anything." He stood up, signaling the end of their conversation.

Robert looked up at Maximilian and lowered his voice to a near whisper. "We need your help. As I said, her problem is not just the drug and alcohol addiction. As you suspect, these are responses to something else, something much deeper."

Maximilian reacted angrily. "Don't bullshit me. I'm not playing games with you or her. Sophie is in very serious psychological trouble."

"Please," Robert said. "Please hear me out." Maximilian just looked at him. He decided that he didn't like or trust this evasive man.

Robert stood and faced Maximilian. "It's important that you listen," Robert spoke with authority now. The change in Robert's tone was not lost on the doctor. Maximilian sat down and looked only at Robert, wondering what revelation might come next.

"Dr. Maxwell, although Sophie needs clinical help, she cannot stay here. It is dangerous for her to remain here." He lowered his voice again and added, "There are people looking for her. Dangerous people. She must be relocated immediately."

"What exactly are you asking me to do?"

"Help us help her." Robert radiated innocence, intelligence and caring.

"And how can I do that?"

"She is leaving with us tomorrow." "What?" Maximilian was incredulous.

Robert continued. "Please forget that she was ever a patient here. There must be nothing in this hospital that documents that she was here." Robert paused briefly, then continued without flinching. "You must remove her records from your files." Robert had spoken with the quiet assurance of someone who knows that he will get what he wants.

Maximilian restrained a guffaw. "Assuming that she wants to go with you, I can't do that. It's illegal to destroy hospital records. How can you even suggest such a thing?"

From his right jacket pocket, Robert extracted a small envelope and let some photographs spill out onto Maximilian's desk. The pictures were of Sophie, the present pope, *a cardinal and some characters who looked like thugs*. "You must help us, doctor," he said. "Sophie's dreams of the people following her, coming here to get her, are not delusions." Maximilian picked up the pictures and looked at them, puzzled about their significance.

"They are as real as you and I, Dr. Maxwell." Robert spoke with sincere conviction and concern. "These are only some of the people who are looking for Sophie. There will be others. They will come here looking for information about her. She was involved with some unscrupulous characters in a few shady business deals. As I said, these men are dangerous. It is not only for Sophie's sake that we are asking you to destroy the records. It is in the best interest of everyone who has had contact with her here. You might also want to consider the risks to yourself and your own family."

"My family?" Maximilian looked up at Robert with surprise and distaste. Silas was watching the scene with interest.

"I understand that your wife died of cancer and left you with two young daughters. We were so sorry to hear about your misfortune. Surely there has been enough grief in your life already." Robert spoke the words with little compassion.

Maximilian put the photographs down and spoke soberly. His concern was first for the patient. "What has Sophie done?"

"It's not only what she's done, Dr. Maxwell. It's what she knows," Robert said as he retrieved the photos and returned them to his pocket.

"Why should I believe you? Why should I accept what you're telling me? I don't know even who you are. You could be the ones hunting her." The counselor was beginning to worry about his children. All his life, he had been strong willed but hearing that his daughters could be in danger made him realize just how weak he could be.

"We will do Sophie no harm. You must believe me.

We've come here to help her. It isn't safe for her to be here anymore."

"This woman is in a fragile state of mind. If she doesn't continue to receive care, she could wind up dead, maybe by her own hand. Do you understand what I'm saying?" *Maximilian spoke with urgency.*

Robert leaned across the desk and put his face close to Maximilian's. "Let me repeat what I said, Dr.

Maxwell. We are here to help her. We have no intention of hurting her or letting her be harmed in any way. And we don't want you or your family to suffer any more than you already have. We are simply asking for your cooperation. The *people who appear in her dreams* are most likely on their way to Vermont right now."

FIVE

Brattleboro
June 5

Robert and Sophie leave the Institute together

The sun was playing *cat and mouse* with an uncertain sky as two men and a woman sped through the front gates of Hope House. Robert was alone in the front seat of a new rental car. He had spent the previous afternoon making preparations for their escape and was fairly certain they would be able to leave the country without incident. He had checked and rechecked every detail in his mind. And just to be sure, he was doing it again.

In the back seat, Jamie was busy telling Sophie how Robert had convinced Dr. Maxwell to destroy her files, but she was having trouble paying attention to him. Her records had been burned before they left Maximilian's office, he said. For the moment at least, no one knew where she had been, where she was, or who she was with.

On the ride, the three talked a great deal about how they had been separated from each other in Europe by the organization and how diabolical it had become. Then they discussed their exit plans to make sure that everyone knew what to do. Once finished, Sophie and Jamie napped in the back seat.

Robert thought that Sophie seemed more coherent and energetic than when they had first turned up in Brattleboro, and happy to be reunited with them. But she was also mood swinging. At times she seemed alert, then listless and withdrawn, and she was easily agitated. Robert desperately needed for her to be well but could see that she did need time to heal. He hoped a few months would be enough.

Rain had begun to fall lightly on the windshield of the car as they passed under the sign directing them towards Route 90 and Boston. But they didn't turn. Robert made it a policy never to leave from the same airport he flew into and continued driving south. Their destination was Bradley International Airport in Winsor Locks, Connecticut. There, a plane was waiting to take them up to Canada. They were going to *a rural convent* where Sophie *would be well taken care of.*

SIX

Paris, France
July 10

***A Sister Superior knows all about
the head of the Opus Dei***

The Church of Saint-Germain des Pres is located in the 6th arrondissement of Paris. The convent close to there was a residence for many nuns of the order including Sister Mary Bernadette. The rooms were quite modest with only a bed, phone and a microwave.

For years now Mary Bernadette had been responsible for many church affairs and overseeing selected unusual operations including financial matters.

The phone in her room rang at just past eleven o'clock in the evening and she wearily answered it.

"Hello, Sister Mary," the man said in English.

Sister Mary sat up. "What time is it?" She immediately recognized her superior's voice.

"I have something I need you to do," the voice said. "I just received a call from an influential American Archbishop. Perhaps you know of him, Manuel Zagranski?"

"The head of the Opus Dei? Of course I know of him. Who in the Church doesn't?" Sister Mary answered. Thinking quickly about the man she knew the Archbishop's conservative prelature had grown powerful in recent years. *Their ascension to grace was jump-started in 1982 when Pope John Paul II unexpectedly elevated them to a personal prelature of the Pope,* officially sanctioning all of their practices. Suspiciously, Opus Dei's elevation occurred the same year the wealthy sect allegedly had *transferred one billion dollars into the Vatican's Institute for Religious Works* – commonly known as the Vatican Bank – *bailing it out* of an embarrassing *bankruptcy*. In a second maneuver that raised eyebrows the Pope placed the founder of Opus Dei on the "fast track" for sainthood, accelerating an often century-long waiting period for canonization to a mere twenty years. Sister Mary could not help but feel that the Opus Dei's good standing in Rome was suspect, but one did not argue with the Holy See.

"Archbishop Zagranski called to ask me a favor," the voice told her, sounding nervous. "One of the Opus Dei numeraries is in Paris tonight...."

As Sister Mary listened to the odd request, she felt a deepening confusion. "I'm sorry; you say this visiting Opus Dei numerary cannot wait until morning?"

"I'm afraid not. His plane leaves very early. He has always dreamed of seeing the church," the voice told her.

"But it's far more spectacular by day," Sister Mary told him.

"I would consider it a favor if you would let him in tonight," the voice told her. "He can be there in twenty minutes."

"Of course," Sister Mary answered dutifully.

Puzzled, Sister Mary remained for a moment in bed pondering the odd request. Her sixty-two year old body was tired and painful. Opus Dei had always made her uneasy. Beyond its prelature adherence to the arcane ritual of corporeal mortification, their views on women were poor at best. She had been shocked to learn that female numeraries were forced to clean the men's toilets for no pay while the men were at vespers; women were forced to sleep on bare floors, while the men on comfortable mats; and women were forced to endure additional requirements of corporeal mortification as an added penance for their sins. Unbelievably, while most of the Catholic Church was gradually moving in the right direction with respect to women's rights, the Opus Dei was impeding the progression. But, Sister Mary had to obey her orders.

Getting up uneasily, she felt a rush of pain from her feet and then an uncomfortable wave of panic. As a follower of God, Sister Mary had learned to find joy in her own soul. Tonight though, those feelings were missing. Ignoring her own fears, she went quickly to let the Opus Dei visitor into the church.

SEVEN

Jerusalem
September 22

Silas chases after the secret for the
head of the brotherhood

It didn't take those directing the Opus Dei long to figure out what had probably happened to the missing treasure. Deciding what to do about it, however, had taken years.

The intense disagreements in the 1960s between Pope Paul VI and Monsignor Josemaria Escriva de Balaguer had created a major rift in the church. It was Pope Paul VI's fervent hope to diplomatically establish a worldwide inter-religious coalition. Escriva's vision was diametrically opposed to this: He was obsessed with the creation of an ambitious central committee that would not only govern the church but would direct it in increasing its influence worldwide, especially in the developing nations, using the technology and the information industry. Escriva's book, *The Cronica,* warned against atheists and "evil forces of nature" that might misuse this technology to subvert the control of the Catholic Church.

The Opus Dei priests who discovered the fake relic assumed it must have been the work of Pope Paul VI and his followers, probably around the time of Paul VI's journey to the Holy Land in the early 1960s. The organization had kept detailed records of Paul's every move and it was a simple task to piece together a reasonable scenario. But what their computers could not tell them was where Pope Paul VI had taken the priceless icon or where it was now.

In response to a call from the Opus Dei in Rome, Silas Willoughby took an early afternoon flight from Maine to New York. In the airport lounge, the steely-eyed Yankee met briefly with his contact and then boarded a nearly full TWA 747 for Jerusalem. After a 10-hour flight, the aircraft began its descent to Ben Gurion Airport in Tel Aviv, screeching onto the runway at 8:25 in the morning and taxiing to a stop some 200 yards from the only building in sight. A raspy voice on the intercom told him that the temperature was 91 degrees and that heavy rains had been forecast but were no longer expected. The steward wished them all a safe and enjoyable stay in Israel and thanked them for flying with TWA.

When he exited the aircraft, a blast of hot air hit Silas, an uncomfortable sensation that was a far cry from the early autumn chill he had left behind in Maine. He moved slowly down the gateway steps and walked to the shuttle bus that spewed clouds of blue smoke into the air as it waited to take passengers to the immigration terminal. Like most Middle Eastern airports, the Ben Gurion was grey and ungarnished with no welcome signs and few attempts to make it look inviting. Immigration and customs clearance took the passengers almost two hours and then to make matters worse, it seemed that the car rental agency had somehow lost his reservation. Silas fixed the problem by behaving like a terribly obnoxious tourist and was on his way within an hour.

The name on his airline tickets, passport, credit cards and rental agreement was Dr. Silas Whitlock. Repeating "Whitlock, Silas Whitlock," he drove east towards the mountains and Jerusalem. He took little notice of the historic vistas all around him, concentrating more on the names of the people he would be meeting shortly at the hotel.

Forty minutes later, he pulled up to the Jerusalem Hilton.

"Are you here for the medical conference, sir?" a young bellhop asked.

"Yes. My name is Dr. Silas Whitlock," Silas said cordially.

"Should I park the car in the underground garage, sir?"

"Yes and I'll need help with my bags"

The hotel's exterior was gaudy, with an unforgivably elaborate glass entrance, and Silas entered disdainfully. As soon as he was inside, a large woman greeted him loudly.

"Silas! How good to see you again! How was your flight? I'm so glad you could make it to the conference this year."

Accepting her forced embrace, Silas cursed her silently for her breath, which smelled strongly of fish. "The flight was fine! You're looking well, Candice." He grimaced and took her fleshy arm in his.

"We're all here now. It's so exciting! Why don't you hurry up and check in, so we can have that drink you promised me two years ago."

Silas understood. She would shortly bring him up to date. He hoped she and the rest of the team had found a lead to the relic.

"After you've gotten yourself settled in, give me a call. I'm in Room 718. I'll let the others know you've arrived. And by the way, I took the liberty of pre-registering you for the convention. Your materials are up in my room." Her smile was lavish and her grip just a little too tight.

Silas filled out the hotel registration forms at the front desk, then went with the bellhop up to the 10th floor. In less than 10 minutes, Candice and two others from the Opus Dei arrived at his room. "There is much to be done," Candice said as she closed the door and began the introductions.

EIGHT

September 23

Silas is hostile to the nun
The Dead Sea Scrolls, Aleppo Codex and Apocrypha

Early the next morning, Silas was *startled awake*. *A nun* in a black and white habit hovered so close to him that he could feel the heat of her breath on his face. She was Sister Mary Bernadette, his sixth grade teacher. It was 1966 and he was back at St. Mary's in Bath, Maine. Mary Bernadette stood over him, brandishing a yardstick and asking him the same questions over and over again.

"Who made you?" she demanded.

"God made me!" he answered.

"And why did God make you?" she pressed.

"I don't know!" Silas's answer was always the same. The ruler smashed down upon the knuckles of his outspread hands as the sister shouted, "God made you in His own image to love and to serve Him!" She struck him again but Silas remained silent, wondering why it was so important that he repeat her exact words and vowing to get even with her.

He rose, shaken and sweating and the bloody image vanished. He was glad the bitch was finally dead. It was the first time in years that he had thought about St. Mary's and he made a mental note of it. Reading the *Jerusalem Post* over breakfast an hour later, his mind made the connection. It was Candice. Beneath the make-up and perfume, she looked an awful lot like Sister Mary Bernadette.

Relieved, he finished breakfast quickly and went to the front desk to exchange his dollars for shekels. "Would you be kind enough to point me in the direction of the Israel Museum?" he asked the clerk as he handed her the money. "I'd like to see the *Dead Sea Scrolls*." The girl counted the Israeli currency into his outstretched hand, talking into a telephone before turning her attention back to him. "If you drive directly out of the parking lot and then turn right, the museum is a mile down on the right."

"Thank you. That seems simple enough." Silas gave her an appreciative smile, thinking she was rather attractive, pocketed the money and walked through the revolving doors to the parking area. Five minutes later, he had found the museum. He parked among the tour buses, slipped through a pack of Japanese tourists, and entered the first small building. In the gift shop, he bought a museum guide book, then ambled down the stone walkway, reading about the discovery of *the seven Dead Sea Scrolls in 1947 in a cave in Qumran, near Jericho and the Dead Sea and about 50 kilometers from Jerusalem.* The scrolls had been found inside jars that protected them from the humidity, a practice which was described in the Bible and *the Apocrypha*. Qumran was known for being terribly arid.

Wandering through the grounds, he reached the round building called the Shrine of the Book. Inside, its stone walls were dotted with display cases describing the famous papers. Lights flicked on and off in the cases at 30-second intervals, triggered by buttons on the front panels. He pushed the button on the case in front of him and the light flashed on. "The *Aleppo Codex* is the earliest known *Hebrew manuscript*. The one here in Israel contains 295 of the original 487 leaves."

He moved along with the crowd to the next case. A tourist inadvertently bumped against him and he spun around, prepared to deliver a blow, and saw the startled eyes of an old lady looking up at him. Apologizing pro-fusely, he calmed her and her friends with a few soothing words and then turned his attention back to the glass case. "The Manuscript of Discipline allows into its membership only those who pledge themselves to follow the laws of God given through Moses and through all of His servants and prophets," he read.

He shuffled on. "The War of the Sons of Light Against the Sons of Darkness. These scrolls outline the procedures and participants in the future *Apocalyptic War*." Silas wondered who would be on each side.

Finally, he reached the center display, which was *shaped on the top like the rods holding the Torah*. On November 23, 1947, Professor Eleazar Sukenik from Hebrew University had been approached by an Armenian antiquities dealer who showed him a scrap from a leather scroll and told him that while looking for a stray goat near the *Dead Sea*, a group of Bedouins had wandered into a cave and discovered a cache of ancient scrolls. Five days later, as the United Nations debated the future of Palestine; Sukenik had followed the trader to an attic in Bethlehem and viewed the *scrolls*. He arranged to take three of them to Jerusalem for authentication. The *scrolls contained psalm-like poems,* a partial text of the *Book of Isaiah*, and an *apocalyptic* work about a future military struggle. Four similar scrolls had been acquired by the Syrian Orthodox Monastery of Saint Mark *in Jerusalem* and put up for sale in the U.S., but no buyers had been found and the scrolls had mysteriously disappeared shortly thereafter.

In 1953, Sukenik's son, Yigael Yadin, was lecturing on the *Dead Sea Scrolls* at Columbia University when an acquaintance, a reporter for the *Wall Street Journal,* told him that the four scrolls had resurfaced and were available for purchase. Yadin had successfully negotiated for them through a banker friend, Samuel Gottesman.

A man calling himself the Metropolitan had sold the scrolls to Gottesman for $250,000. The next morning, they had all been transferred from a vault at the Waldorf Astoria to the offices of the Israeli consulate. Within days, they were sent on to Jerusalem and reunited with the three that Sukenik had studied.

As Silas read, he looked around casually to make sure he was not being observed by potential adversaries or relic seekers. Satisfied that he was not, he turned back to the Temple Scroll, trying to read the tiny lettering. Minutes later, he removed his eyeglasses and rubbed his eyes to relieve the rapidly building pressure in his head. He took one last look around the building and then headed out. It was time to find Jaffa Street and the entrance to the Old City.

Jerusalem gleamed in the late morning sun. Seeing the Tower of David to his right, Silas trudged up the steep stone road leading to Jaffa Gate, passing the Museum of David, which he recognized from a guidebook description. A crowd of soldiers milled around the entrance to a small square and he moved past them into the square, glancing into a series of small shops along the way. Inside, more soldiers lined the perimeter. Trying to look as though he knew where he was going, he wandered through the streets and passageways until he came to an arched stone entry which looked like the way into the famous Old City.

"Come see what I have for you, I promise you will find nothing like it anywhere," a merchant harangued him, momentarily blocking his path down the steep stones of David Street.

"No, thank you," Silas said, pushing him away gently. A little farther on, three more men approached him. "Please come in and see what you like," they said, each one trying to lure him into his shop. He ignored them all and pushed forward.

After a minute of walking in no particular direction, he paused to get his bearings and wipe beads of sweat from his brow. The street opposite him was called the

Street of Herbs, but the name meant nothing to him and he couldn't find it on his guide map.

"You are an American?" Jet black hair curled around the scarred face of a boy standing in front of him. Although he was only 13 years old or so, he had the posture and gait of an old man, hunched and limping badly. Yet he wore a well-polished smile and his eyes sparkled gaily.

"Yes, I am. Why?"

"Do you want a tour of the city? I am Achmed, a very smart guide. Much experienced. Not expensive at all." His English was moderately acceptable.

"What is 'not expensive?'" Silas answered him slightly annoyed by the intrusion.

"Seventy-five shekels. I will show you the whole city for only 75 shekels. Three hours' time."

"Too much, too expensive." Dismissing him, Silas headed down a narrow street to the right.

"No, no, American. Nothing down there." Achmed limped quickly after him.

"How do you know where I'm going?" Silas eluded two jewelry merchants and paused to look back at Achmed.

"Everything of importance is the other way." The boy looked amused. He knew how difficult it was for strangers to find their way in the maze of the Old City.

Silas stumbled as two soldiers pushed him aside, and then replied, "OK, I'll give you 50 shekels and no more. I want you to take me to the Christian Quarter, to the Church of the Holy Sepulcher, and no tricks." His tone reflected his strong irritation at the clumsiness of the soldiers.

"Sixty shekels," Achmed insisted, extending his hand for payment.

"Fifty and that's all, take it or leave it." Silas began to walk away from the boy.

"OK, 50 shekels," Achmed agreed. "Business is bad for everyone in the city. I take 50 shekels for the tour. But I give only two hours' time, not three." He held out his hand for the money but Silas said, "I'll pay you when you get me there."

They reversed direction and walked back to a cross street. The youngster talked incessantly as they climbed to another street, which looked suspiciously like one Silas thought he had already been on. Ten minutes later, at the end of Al-Wad Road, Achmed stopped. "This is the fourth station, where Jesus met His mother. The third station is down here."

Achmed walked them through a group of somber pilgrims who were praying and then, standing with difficulty on his toes, pointed to a wall carving three feet above them. "This is where Jesus fell for the first time." He smiled with satisfaction, clearly pleased with his vast knowledge of the Holy City. The carving portrayed Christ falling to His knees in pain on the hard rock steps, the Cross of Crucifixion upon his shoulders.

"I told you to take me to the Christian Quarter. I'm not here for the 10-penny tour. I want to go to the church, now."

The smile on the boy's face faded. "We go up the steps this way, along the Via Dolorosa, the Sorrowful Way."

The Path of Sorrows, Silas had already read, was considered the most sacred road in the world by many

Christians. Along its uneven path, the Son of God had been led from His condemnation by Pilate to His crucifixion and death on the rocky hill of Golgotha. Silas could feel his agitation increase. He was not interested in recreating the journey of Christ. His only desire was to find the ancient basilica and the priests who, he hoped, would direct him closer to the missing relic.

"This is the seventh station." Achmed could not contain himself and pointed briefly to his left to a Roman column in an old Franciscan chapel. "It is called Judgment Gate. Christ fell here for the second time." Achmed again quickened his pace.

"How much further?"

The boy turned his head slightly to answer him, realizing it was useless to try to interest Silas in Jerusalem's history. "One minute's time only."

The last section of the Via Dolorosa opened onto a small marketplace with only a few vendors. At the far end, a small doorway framed in old timbers with a simple metal sign led into the courtyard of the Church of the Holy Sepulcher.

One might think that the place where Jesus was crucified would be a sanctified religious monument, enshrined in beauty and radiance. But the Church of the Holy Sepulcher was nothing more than a dingy 12th-century slum of a building whose rock foundation was crumbling away into dirt.

"This is the place where Jesus was killed," Achmed said. "There are many religions in this church, maybe about six in all. There are the Catholics, the Armenian

Apostolics, the Greek Orthodox, and the Coptics. The Muslims are responsible for opening the doors. The church needs some fixing. They will repair it once they all can agree how to. They have to come together to do it. It's God's law. It's God's wish."

Silas followed the boy down three stone steps, noticing the graffiti written all over the rotting doors. Achmed pointed to his right, saying, "This is the tenth station, where Jesus was stripped of His clothes."

"Where is Calvary? And where was the cross of Jesus found?" Silas asked.

"At the top of the stairs, in front, in the Place of the Skull. That is the site of the Crucifixion. Down below, in back of the church, that's where the cross was found." The boy pointed up to his right as he spoke.

"Both sites are inside the church?"

"Yes and no. There are two shrines. One is in front and extends out here and the other is in back and down below." The boy pointed to the chapel at the top of the stairs, not knowing whether he should continue and show Silas the last of the stations.

"Take me to the site of the Crucifixion first."

They walked in and pushed their way past a group of tourists who were gazing up at the ceiling. Silas looked up, then down, surprised at the extent of the neglect. The place smelled musty, stale. Dust floated around them like an unwanted mist, the residue of the rotting beams above.

"This is the Stone of the Anointment, the 13th station." The boy directed Silas's attention to a single stone slab in the entrance. "That is where Christ was anointed." About six feet long and two feet wide, the stone was raised a foot from the floor and framed by tarnished gold on three sides. Unlit candles surrounded it. "It's called the Anointment Stone," Achmed said.

A woman in black forced her way past them and fell to her knees, wailing and kissing the stone slab repeatedly, begging for God's forgiveness. She looked penniless, exhausted and meek.

"Where's Calvary?" Silas snapped.

"The 10th, 11th and 12th stations are up the stairs." The boy took the lead, turning every now and then to make sure Silas was still behind him, and led him to two altars built on the right side of Golgotha. The altar on the far right had been given to the Franciscans, the one on the left to the Greek Orthodox Church. Above each was a dark, depressive mural. Climbing higher, they reached the Latin Chapel of the Franciscans, home of the 10th and 11th stations. Here, the floor was brilliantly decorated with glossy mosaics, and colorful paintings hung on the walls. Lights danced above a marble altar and streamed from small candles in well-polished gold candelabra, making the drab stations below seem even more neglected.

Silas surveyed the first altar. The emotional atmosphere here was different than below. He was captivated by his environment against his will. Gazing into the candlelight, he tried to purge himself of the distracting sensations.

"Do you want to buy candles to light at the altar?" Achmed asked, completely unaffected by anything. Sensing resistance, he resumed his lecture about the altars. "The gold altar marks the site of the 11th station, where Jesus was nailed to the cross." Icons depicted Christ, the Blessed Virgin and St. John.

The chapel was brilliantly lit by oil lamps and candles. Uncountable fresh flowers scented the air and beneath a life-size statue of Jesus, an old man in a shabby woolen jacket stooped over them, replacing the wilted ones with fresh ones and changing the water in their vases.

"It was here," Achmed continued, in duet with an Italian priest talking to his parishioners, "where the crosses of Jesus and the two thieves were. An earthquake opened a large fissure in the bedrock below on the day Christ was put to death. It was the wrath of God that caused the tremor. This is the epicenter of all of the world's energy portals. Here is a source of incredible power, the gateway to Heaven and Hell." Achmed recited the words matter-of-factly, hobbling closer to the altar.

A *silver disk* lay beneath the center of the marble altar. A *hole cut in its center* allowed visitors to touch and kiss the Rock of Calvary, where the Cross had been put into the ground. Touching this rock was the reason why Silas had come here. He had been told by his contacts at the hotel to put his hand and lips on the Rock of Calvary three times as a signal to the priests there. Agitated and impatient, Silas elbowed aside the man whose job was to wipe the disc clean after every visitor. Dropping down to his knees and failing to fold his hands in prayer, he unemotionally kissed and then touched the sacred stone twice.

It was when he kissed the stone the third time that Silas became dizzy and lost his balance. Struggling to regain control, he stood up and squared his shoulders and chin. "Where is the site of the Finding of the Holy Cross?" he demanded of Achmed.

"Down those stairs, in back of the church." The boy pointed to his left.

"Take me there." An unaccountable sense of uneasiness came over Silas as they descended the stairs.

"Be careful of the loose rocks on the steps," Achmed cautioned.

At the bottom, their progress was interrupted by 12 Franciscan friars walking in procession, all carrying candles. Their pace was tedious and their chant of praise to the Lord was monotonous. Achmed and Silas pushed themselves against a wall and stayed out of the way. As the last friar passed, Silas noticed a large African in priestly robes looking at him from the back of the church. Once he knew Silas saw him, he vanished down the stairs to the grotto.

Sunlight twinkled through cracked panes of stained glass, partially lighting the way as Silas and Achmed walked to the grotto. It was here that the Cross had been excavated in 1965. The chanting of the priests faded as they approached a set of stairs not unlike the steps leading to the Crucifixion altars, uneven slabs of stone worn away by the feet of hundreds of thousands of pilgrims.

On the second step, Silas slipped. "Are you feeling all right?" An older man caught him.

"Yes, thank you. I just lost my footing, that's all," Silas responded abrasively. But when he tried to move he realized that he was dizzy and had broken into a cold sweat.

"Why don't you sit for a second and catch your breath." Achmed and the stranger helped him. "The stairs are steep and the way winding," the man murmured. Silas, who was shivering, knew he should be highly alert now but found himself sluggish.

Achmed stood on the step below as several others gathered around to offer sympathy and assistance. The black priest was there now. "Is there anything I can do?" he asked, in a voice unusually deep and calm.

"He seems to be a bit woozy."

"Perhaps you should lie down then." He put his arm around Silas's shoulder, gently supporting him.

"No, I'm fine. Please, just give me a minute and I'll be all right."

"This is not an uncommon occurrence here. The basilica is a very emotional place. Why don't we take you to the sacristy for a short rest? Come, there is a place where you can lie down." He helped Silas up the steps, accompanied by the older man, whose accent was English, and Achmed, who was wishing he had collected his fee earlier.

In a matter of minutes, they were making their way through the crowds at the various stations. Achmed was silent as they passed the last one, the Shrine of the Holy Sepulcher, where the Son of God had been buried and risen from the dead. Just behind it, at the Syrian

Orthodox Chapel, two priests were pressuring a young tourist to buy cheap mementos.

"Lie here for a moment and we'll send for a doctor," the priest said when they arrived at the Franciscan Chapel of the Blessed Sacrament. He helped Silas onto a narrow wooden bench.

"Don't send for anyone, please," Silas said with all the conviction he could muster. "I'll be all right in a minute. I assure you, I don't need a doctor."

Within minutes they were joined by four friars from the sacristy. "What have we here?" inquired an elderly priest, kind eyes shining out from a web of wrinkles.

"This young man became dazed on the steps leading down to the grotto, Father," the black priest answered.

"Is he ill?"

"I'm not sure, Father. He asks that we not call a doctor."

Silas directed his attention to the leathery-faced Franciscan. "I'm feeling fine now, Father. Really, there's no need to send for anyone. Thank you for your kindness. I'll be leaving in a minute."

They all stood in silence. Silas tried to focus but the dizziness persisted. "I'll be fine in a minute," he repeated unconvincingly. "Please, don't bother anyone else. I'm embarrassed enough as it is."

Father James looked down at him and in a paternal voice said, "There is no need to be embarrassed, Mr. Willoughby. We are all brothers here."

Silas was startled by the sound of his real name being spoken. But Father James, dignified in his flowing robes, just touched his shoulder gently.

"Sit, Silas, and rest. You don't look well. You're safe here with us. Our brothers from the Opus Dei called us. We knew you were coming and we know about the lost treasure. We want to help you get it back."

NINE

Jerusalem
September 24

A misguided soul of the Opus Dei —
a 'lone assassin'

Silas left Jerusalem on Route 1 east, the same road he had taken in from the airport, then turned north on Route 90.

The road took him first past Jericho and then Qumran, where the famous scrolls had been found. He was tempted to stop and investigate the sheep herders' cave but doggedly kept on the road to Tabgha, where he had been told he would find a priest named Father Leigh Rovarik.

He arrived in the village as the sun was beginning its initial decline. According to one of his reference books, *The Land of Jesus,* he was approaching the Church of the Multiplication. "There had been only five loaves of bread and two fishes," he read, one eye on the page, the other on the dirt road, "when Jesus fed the thousands who listened to Him preach in the fields that surrounded the little town of Tabgha." Silas didn't care if the poor had been fed here or what they had eaten. His mission was to investigate the man who had been the rector at the time of Pope Paul VI's visit many years ago.

The Church of the Multiplication was nothing like the decrepit church in the Old City. Silas had read that the small structure before him was a reconstruction of the original church, which had been destroyed by earthquakes in the sixth and seventh centuries. As he entered it, he noticed a simple cross and plaque above the front door commemorating the calamities. Inside, it was impeccably clean, well cared for and brightly lit. Rows of chairs extended out from the central altar and simple white pillars lined the sides of the main section. He took note of the fact that he was alone in the building.

He walked down the nave towards an unadorned altar and looked intently at a round object hanging by a single wire some 20 feet above him. It appeared to be made of iron. The lights of its 12 mounted candles reflected throughout the church.

Ignoring the sign that said *Do Not Enter,* he walked up to the altar. A colorful floor mosaic surrounded a large rock that protruded from the floor. The mosaic depicted the miracle of replenishment, the name given to the miraculous multiplication of loaves of bread and fishes, when Jesus fed the multitudes.

From out of nowhere, a priest approached and stood with him before the altar. "Beautiful, isn't it?" he asked, looking into Silas's eyes.

"Yes, it is." Silas was getting used to steady gazes from strange priests.

"Where are you from, my son?" the priest asked.

The white-bearded man seemed to be indulging in some type of idle conversation. Knowing who he probably was, Silas lied to him. "I'm from New York, Father, here on holiday to visit the Holy Shrines."

"How long will you stay in Israel?" The priest blessed himself and began to walk down the steps. Then he turned and motioned for Silas to go with him towards a side door.

"I'm not sure, Father. A few days, maybe a week. It depends on how long my money lasts."

The priest laughed at the textbook response. Chatting casually, he and Silas walked out to the courtyard and seated themselves on a bench, from which Silas pretended to admire the landscape.

"What have you seen so far that is of interest to you?" the priest asked.

"I enjoyed the Church of the Holy Sepulcher," Silas answered.

"What is happening to the church is a sin." "It does need some work."

"It needs a lot of work." The priest was blunt.

"It's strange that you speak so freely to a stranger, Father. Would some not say that your directness is more than a little outspoken?"

"I care not what people think, young man. I have been speaking my mind freely for my entire life. I'm too old to change now." He paused and then continued. "Maybe the church has the same problems. Maybe it also is too old to change. I find that these things come slower as you age. Everything in life falls into patterns and if we are not careful, even what is wrong can become comfortable. It is very hard to alter old ways. Especially when the people responsible do not want to, when they are content to do nothing but watch the crumbling walls of the holy church turn into dust. It is sad to see the church that was once so strong, alive and vibrant wasting away into nothingness."

"I'm getting the feeling that we're not talking about just one church in the Old City of Jerusalem."

The priest rose, looking silently out over the distant hills and the tiny *sheep* wandering among the olive trees.

"Many wise and brave men have walked these mountains before us, thinking many of these same thoughts, my son, trying to do what has to be done. But the wolves wear the clothing of the lambs." His expression had become grave and his shriveled face no longer bore a smile.

Neither man said a word for the next few minutes as they stood together, feeling the warm highland winds blow over the lilies and wildflowers dotting the fields below them.

"I received a phone call last night from friends in Jerusalem," the priest finally said. "They told me that someone was coming here to find me, to ask questions I probably should be afraid of." He raised his eyebrows, turning his attention back to Silas.

Silas was expressionless. "What kind of questions, Father?"

"It seems that some people in Rome are very interested in a conversation I had here with Pope Paul VI in 1964." He smiled.

"You met with Pope..." Silas said, trailing off his words to encourage the priest to continue.

"It seems the people in Rome are missing something from their coffers."

"What's missing, Father?" he responded innocently.

"Something that is not theirs, my son. Something that will never be theirs."

Silas decided to break his masquerade. "You are Father Leigh Rovarik, are you not?"

"Yes I am, my son. And you are not simply a tourist on holiday, are you now?"

"No, I'm not, Father. I'm the one who has been sent to ask you the questions that do not make you afraid."

His faded brown robes flapping in the breeze, Rovarik led Silas towards the rectory. "Fine," he said softly. "Then let's make life easy on each other, shall we?

Now that we each know who the other is and we both realize you have come a very long way to find me, let's go to my office and talk. I doubt that I can influence your reasons for coming here. And I have no money with which to pay you, like those in Rome do. It matters little now if I can convince you that the pope came to see me for all the right reasons and that the people who hired you are the ones he warned me about."

The two were again silent for a moment before the priest continued. "You see, my son, it was because of

Monsignor Escriva and the Opus Dei that the Holy Father came here."

The old man had quickly assessed Silas as strong willed, skilled and possessing a sharp tongue, but terribly *misguided*. As he faced the mercenary, his expression was solemn. Something in his tone and manner made Silas more than a little uneasy.

"We really don't want to hurt you. But be careful! You are walking on hallowed ground here. *The treasure you seek* is not here anymore. It has been removed. And I won't help you find it. Believe what I tell you, or don't, Silas Willoughby. It doesn't really matter. God is in control of what will happen now."

TEN

St. Thomas, Ontario
October 12

The Opus Dei, Knights and the Vatican are linked
There is an Old Catholic Hierarchy
and a New Order Plan

Sophie awoke just before sunrise, stirred by the sound of someone singing. Rising, she thanked God for another day of not waking up in fear and for more time to get healthy and clear. Listening to the melody coming from the next cell, she stretched and rested her gaze on the plain wooden cross hanging from a nail in the wall opposite her. Involuntarily, she superimposed upon it the body of Jesus and thought about what it must have been like to endure His pain. In comparison, hers was insignificant. She wondered, why did there have to be such anguish in the world?

Rejoicing in the beauty of feeling clearheaded, she opened the window and felt a rush of cool air come in. In the courtyard below only a few remnants of the abundance of summer greeted her. Dahlias, pansies, roses, all were dying. Rich, waxy beech leaves carpeted the northern corner. She thought that just like the fragrant flowers, everyone should be willing to offer up joyfully their most wonderful gifts before they leave this world. She decided that she wanted to be like a flower from now on. Sweet fragrances teased her and vanished as she raised her eyes to the brilliant sky and once again gave thanks for the moment's pleasure. All around her, birds chirped stubbornly, their fragile nests perched on bare branches, as they loudly voiced their songs of joy for one more day.

In the distance, the highlands gleamed, their peaks covered with white snow. They reminded Sophie of her childhood days in Switzerland. Feeling a cold chill rush through her, she abruptly shut the window. As she rubbed her arms to get warm, a description she had once read about cocoons came back to her: "A cocoon is a covering, usually spun of a silk-like filament, woven around the central origin of a life system for protection during its development. It protects the immature organism from outside interventions and attacks." Sophie had spun a silk web of her own, an intricate covering to shield herself from the people and thoughts she feared, and it had almost killed her.

She looked down at the cot, a symbol of a simpler life. Robert had been right to take her to the convent. She needed to be here. Putting her palms together, she said a prayer of thanks for the Sisters of the Holy Angels and one asking God for forgiveness and strength.

A soft knock at the door was followed by the entrance of the woman who had become her new protector and a true friend. Sister Julien Taylor was not a typical nun. She was very young and very beautiful, with pronounced cheekbones, deep-set hazel eyes and a proud, muscular carriage. She reminded Sophie of her mother, tall and self-composed, like a goddess. Never had she been so comfortable with a woman or thought as much about anyone as she did about Julien.

Julien wore white sneakers, pale blue socks, maroon Spandex tights and a beige Champion sweatshirt. Her hair was a medium length, easy to tie up or let down and squeaky clean. She looked nothing like someone who had given her life over to God, especially when she curled her lips into that beloved mischievous pout. Seeing Sophie's sober expression, she spoke in a poorly manufactured Irish brogue. "Are we thinking too much again, Sophie Turrell? I hope you're not still contemplatin' the failures of materialism to provide meanin'ful long-term satisfactions and nourish the emotional and psycho-spirit'l needs of the human heart." Julien leaned back expectantly, hand on her hip.

Sophie tried to match the accent. "No, I'm good Sister Julien. As a matter o' fact, I was thinkin' about the socio-economic impacts of irresponsible corporate capitalism on a rapidly globalizing' economy! And o' what a lovely Monday morning it is!" They shared an embrace and Julien picked up the conversation.

"I looked in on you last night, darling, but you were lost to the world, sleeping like a baby. You were so beautiful I didn't want to disturb you," Julien murmured, brushing Sophie's hair from her face, lingering for a moment.

"How was your trip? I've been worried sick about you. How did the tests go? Which new doctors did you see?"

"Fine, Sophie, my dear. I'll live for awhile. I'll tell you about everything later. Hurry up now and get dressed—we're already behind. Let's not waste time thinking or talking about things we have no control over."

She pulled Sophie up by both hands and left her standing in her shift while she riffled through the one dresser in the room for shorts, socks and sports bra. "We have a life to get ready for, Sophie! There's no time for harping on the condition of this wacky world when we can be enjoying the beauty of the day. We're going for a run!"

Sophie's enthusiasm took a nose dive. They went jogging nearly every morning but she never wanted to do it until they had been on the road for awhile and she'd gotten a second wind. "Where? How far? I'm tired, Julien. Let's skip it today, just today."

Accepting no excuses, Julien persisted. "I thought we'd go up by the big oak tree, around the pond and back by the paved road, about five miles. We have to be here for morning services and after that there are the gardens to get ready for winter, Mother Superior's strict orders."

"Does she still love your running outfit, Julien?" Sophie was being sarcastic.

"We have an understanding about such things, darlin'. You know that."

"I bet you do, Julien. And about some other things, too. I'm sure of it now!"

Julien raised her eyebrows flirtatiously and said nothing more. Sophie knew that the nuns accepted one another on their own merits and were respected as individuals here. Sister Julien had come to the convent after a brilliant career as tennis pro on the international circuit. Her life and game had been interrupted by the discovery of a small tumor on her cerebellum. The doctors were in agreement that surgery was risky, maybe out of the question, and other therapies would not be of much help. She could live for years or die in a few weeks. Trying to prepare herself, Julien had read everything she could about the brain and brain tumors. At the same time she had begun a deep exploration of religion and philosophy, studying Buddhism, the Tao, Native American practices and transcendental meditation. A year later, she had decided to return to Catholicism, the religion of her childhood, and devote her remaining time to more monastic pursuits.

Sophie and Julien had talked a lot about their careers, loves and fears, mostly about their fears and the routes their lives had taken to bring them together here. Their favorite place was Julien's room, with its stacks of books on the desk and all over the floor. The titles included every imaginable subject. Markers and handwritten notes stuck out between pages. Julien read passionately. One night when they were reading together, she had asked Sophie to tell the story of how she had gotten involved with the people she despised so much.

"I was looking for the true meaning of life," Sophie said, her cynicism habitual. "I never really fit into the jet-set world I was born into, but I lived that dead-end existence well into my 20s, thinking it was all there was. Even when I finally rejected it, I had no concept of any real values—I was just trying to get away from what I knew was wrong. You could say I was going through some type of post-adolescent rebellion." Sophie smiled at the thought of her younger self.

"I floated around for years in Europe and then was introduced to Robert at a party in Paris. Robert eventually introduced me to his friends in London, who were all part of a sect, the Opus Dei. Being in the regular church, you probably don't know much about them. But it's an ultra-conservative Catholic movement, very evangelical, and very obsessed with money and power. It was founded in Spain in the 1920s."

Sophie paused to collect her thoughts, then went on. "When we first started dating, I was at a low point in my life, kind of depressed. I was doing what I'd been raised to do and was very busy, but it wasn't satisfying. And Robert had the most beautiful blue eyes I had ever seen. Very soft, loving. He was appealing for a lot of reasons. For one thing, he'd been where I was, despondent, but had pulled himself up and out of it. He was also a little older than me, more mature. And he had a terrific sense of touch. No matter where he touched me, I felt better. I guess I do still love him and I definitely miss all of that. We talked a lot back then, especially about the illusions of life, and Robert got me excited to be alive again. Naturally, as we became intimate, I got to know his friends, eventually joined the organization, and when there was an opening in one of the financial offices of the Opus Dei, I took the job. It was exhilarating. We had projects, goals and each other to focus on."

She made a face when she said "each other," then continued. "It was policy for everyone to go through the ranks or at least be familiar with them, so I had to bring in new members and give talks. And I raised funds. Suffice it to say that we met some amazing financial objectives, Julien." She sighed deeply.

"Looking back on it now, I see Robert was always trying to succeed. He needed the prestige and courted the people in power. He was charismatic, although sometimes chauvinistic, which I suppose was part of his charm. But I could always see his insecure child side. He'd been in the organization for years and was determined to keep moving up. He needed the rush. Not me. I just went along for the ride. I wanted to be part of something that offered some hope and gave me a reason to stay alive. There were others like me too, naive and hopeful, many of whom had been leading boring lives and were looking for something to build a meaningful future on."

Sophie looked to Julien for a response but there was none, just a patient, understanding look. "To us the Catholic Church seemed totally archaic and unresponsive to today's needs. We were the new generation and we had the leaders who knew what they were doing. The old men in Rome, the church hierarchy, they were stuck, not moving forward. They were resistant to even the smallest changes—and we wanted to turn the whole structure on its head. You see, Julien, the founder of Opus Dei, Josemaria Escriva de Balaguer, had outlined an aggressive worldwide evangelical plan. It relied heavily on the assets of people in industry and business, not just on converts and the pennies of the poor who were faithful. He was using their money to accomplish his religious objectives. Money equals success. It was all a very attractive, neat package for me. I thought we were creating something that would really make a difference. We were taking apart the rigid old bureaucracy and the behind-the-times value system and replacing it with leading edge symbols, goals and thoughts. We were redirecting and reconstructing the entire Catholic Church."

Slipping briefly into the brogue she and Julien enjoyed so much, she said, "Fanciful ideas, my dear! But it all became another fucking addiction, another power trip. This time it was a religious power trip and a different financial organization than the one I'd grown up in. But other than that, it was about the same. We own copper mines and plastic companies. They peddle religion. They're all assholes on huge control spins manoeuvring for better playing positions and higher stakes. It was the same kind of thing I'd been trying to get away from."

They were lying on Julien's bed, Sophie at the head, Julien at the foot, their feet entwined. Julien broke lightly into Sophie's monologue, saying, and "Let me guess. You rebelled against the men who managed the money there—and the power—just like you rebelled against your father?"

The thought of her former associates made her overreact. "It's not funny! It may have had many components that were similar, but these guys are serious head cases. I didn't rebel until the end and I should have much earlier. I'd started having some serious doubts about them months before, we all did, but we tucked our concerns away and pretended none of it was happening. Until late last year, when we uncovered some things—policies and procedures that were more than a little unethical. We asked our superiors about the rumors and were told by those pricks that we didn't know enough about anything and should trust them and God to make the right decisions. They talked about love of God and accused us of not understanding faith. We didn't have enough insight, they said. They played on our innocence and guilt and we just backed down."

She took a sip of water and gazed around the room, stopping at a vase of yellow and purple chrysanthemums.

"Those flowers are beautiful," she said. Julien concurred.

"Then I realized that what they were doing was actually stealing money that was supposed to go to needy children. They were using an educational foundation to receive dirty money—and I was one of the directors of it. The foundation was just a front. I started putting two and two together and realized that they were probably dangerous. Awhile back, there had been several mob-style executions of people formerly associated with the Opus Dei. I'm telling you, Julien, these guys are nuts. They're poured from the same mold as those prep

The Brown Code

school bigots I grew up with who run the sweatshops of the world and the do-gooders running the other phony foundations." She breathed deeply. "Some of them wear suits and ties, some wear gold jewelry, others wear black cassocks and white collars. But they're all the same."

Sophie's mind was reeling, remembering how she'd first felt when she'd gotten a glimpse of the criminality of her superiors. "Men are a pain in the ass. They all want the same thing: Their egos expand in direct proportion to their bank accounts, their connections and the women they think they've conquered. And now they want women to act just like them. If it wasn't for Robert and Jamie and a few other good guys, I'd probably put on one of your outfits and join up."

"Calm down!" Julien laughed loudly, breaking the mood, and began puttering with some books, stacking and re-stacking them, balancing them on the overflowing shelves. "Some of us aren't buying in, Sophie! It's not only us nuns. So stop worrying about it. I want to hear more. You figured this stuff out in London?"

"Yeah. I spent almost five years at Shelley House being a good girl and nice to all the right people. I worked in the office of financial operations all week and studied and taught *El Camino* and Escriva's other writings on weekends. I can't believe I did that. What happened to my objectivity? My ability to think for myself? Christ, I'm supposed to know better!"

She rolled over and then sat upright. "But I was very good at both functions. Let me see if I can remember the lectures I used to give youth clubs on the history of the Opus Dei."

Mockingly, she recited her talks, with key changes. "Monsignor Escriva founded the society in Spain in 1928, three years after his ordination as a Roman Catholic priest. By the end of the 1940s the movement had prospered and grown strong—financially and politically—in Spain. Escriva used his influence and money to attract new members from the right wing pro-Catholic Franco government. He eventually opened offices in Rome to be close to the Vatican. Within 30 years the society became a worldwide movement under his direction—with the silent approval of many at the Vatican and the financial support of its self-interested members, many of whom were bankers. Monsignor Escriva died in 1975 after catapulting his doctrine into a powerful force worldwide— especially in the inner circles of the Catholic Church."

Sophie performed a dainty curtsy. Julien clapped, and Sophie continued. "In 1982, with the approval and help of Pope John Paul II, Opus Dei was made *a personal prelature under the new legal framework introduced during the Second Vatican Council in the 1960s*. With Rome's consent, members of the sect owe strict obedience to Opus Dei superiors, both at the Vatican and elsewhere."

Her hand moved to the scar on her right thigh. "I was ecstatic when they invited me to become part of their club. By that time, I'd been near the top for several years but was never allowed to attend certain meetings. Basically, I knew I was being kept out of the important policy-making decisions." She gave a conspiratorial look at Julien. "When I set my mind to it, it didn't take terribly long to maneuver my way up the ladder there. Those so-called gentlemen are incredibly easy to hook if you're smart and know how to get to them. Anyway, I was put in charge of the Dawliffe Educational Foundation and its international finances at an Opus Dei house in London. By then, I was totally absorbed in making money again, even though I thought it was to better serve the cause." She lost herself in a moment of reflection.

"Stealing from the poor to make themselves rich is more like it," she finally said, picking up where she'd left off. "But here's the deal, Julien. I have proof of what they did. *Tapes* of some incriminating meetings. They don't know it yet. At least I don't think they do. But they do know I have records of some illegal transfers of money they made."

Julien sucked in her breath.

"I also have a good deal of their money," Sophie confessed.

"Back up a minute," Julien interrupted. "Where did the coke and other stuff come in?"

"Well, it was an escape. Call it weakness, frustration. Pick an excuse. My friend at the time, a big shot London cardinal, kept it around for me, and it worked, kept me happy and quiet. You know, I'd left my family to get away from these types of money and power circles. And here they were again. These religious people were every bit as sleazy as my father's friends. They were all heartless bastards sitting behind their big desks, living in their selfish worlds."

"What do you mean, you have their money?"

Thinking about her own predicament and future, Sophie didn't answer her directly. "It's not over. I'm not sure it will ever be. Not for me, at least. They're still out there. And I'm here and sober but nothing else has changed. As our great leader Escriva said in *El Camino,* `Remain silent—and you will never regret it. Speak—and you often will.' In taking their money, I spoke, Julien, and they won't be satisfied until they not only get it back but are sure I won't cause any more problems. What I did wasn't exactly sisterly love. But what they'll do to me if they find me is far from brotherly. They're coming after me and they won't stop until they get me."

The conversation was interrupted by the entrance of *Mother Superior*, a stern, buxom woman with a time-worn face. She was dressed in a traditional black-and-white habit and her voice was soft and well-modulated. "Are you ladies coming down to vespers?"

"Yes, we are, Mother Margaret," Julien answered quickly, trying to give Sophie some time to transition back to the convent.

"Good," said Mother Margaret. "Perhaps you can continue your inspirational discussions after services, with the help of some divine guidance that will be imparted to you there."

"I hope so, Mother Superior." Julien nodded her head respectfully as the sister shook her beads before her.

Stopping at the door she looked back at Sophie and said, "It's nice to see you looking so well, Sophie. We're very proud of the progress you've made here in the last few months." Warmth and love radiated from her.

"I couldn't have done it without your help, Mother Margaret. You have all been angels to me."

"We change things by ourselves, child, with the help of others. And we are all angels at one time or another in our lives. Your time will come, my dear, I'm sure of it, if it is not here already."

She addressed Sister Julien next. "God moves us around in mysterious ways. There are always reasons for these things. Sometimes the trials of life are hard to understand, are they not, Sister Julien? It is not easy to accept the reason for the turmoil but the answers are always there if we look hard enough to find them." Again she turned to Sophie and again the energy of her love poured out from her. "God cares for every lamb in equal measure, child. But it is the wandering sheep who returns to the pasture that He loves the most."

ELEVEN

London
October 13

On a busy European street two members
of a brotherhood creep through a gate

A kidnapped captive is trussed
in the back seat of a car

Four bronze lions stood proudly in Trafalgar Square at the base of Lord Nelson's monument as two men walked in from the direction of the National Gallery, deep in conversation, talking about Sophie Turrell. As they did, a set of dark clouds moved over them, lingering stubbornly from the violent storms of the previous night.

The famous square, which was usually busy, was nearly deserted now, except for throngs of pigeons forever pecking at the ground for scraps of food, and a dirty drunkard passed out under a lamppost. Unlike the ominous clouds, the pigeons flew off as the men approached them.

The dampness, fog and drizzle were no more chilling than the conversation taking place. Robert had insisted that they talk in a public place because of the delicate nature of the discussion. The square at dawn was the perfect choice. His companion was Cardinal Carmen Hernandez, the director of Opus Dei's Financial Affairs Central Committee. Carmen, who was doing most of the talking, was strong, elegant and impeccably dressed as usual. His voice was cold as he emphasized the importance of obedience and the strict rules of the organization.

The two men passed the derelict and continued walking to the far corner of the square, where they stopped and glanced casually at the windows and doorways of the buildings across the street.

"We are kinsmen of a sort," Carmen said. "We share an enemy."

"The brotherhood is legendary," Robert replied.

"The brotherhood endures," Carmen said. "Our reach is far and powerful."

"We must insure the item's placement," Robert said. "Solve the code."

"We go back to the 11th Century," Carmen stated. "When the enemy's crusading armies had first pillaged the land as *protectors*."

"Sophie has no respect," said Carmen. "We valued her performance and interpersonal skills but the situation is now totally unacceptable. She is out of control. She's an addict and has been high for months. The last time I saw her she could hardly stand up and she barely recognized me. What she knows could jeopardize our entire effort. She is no longer loyal and cannot be trusted, Robert. Steps must be taken to make sure she causes no more damage." He glanced back towards the museum. "She's dangerous."

Robert's eyes met the cardinal's but he said nothing, so Carmen continued. "Don't be a fool, Robert. The decision has already been made. I advise you to protect your own interests." Robert maintained his composure. He knew the cardinal himself had seen to the reliability of Sophie's drug supply but held his tongue.

"If there was any other way to make sure that she would not use the information, we certainly would consider options. You know that. I am very fond of Sophie, as I know you are. Surely you know you're not the only one who cares about her. But that's not the issue," Carmen said.

"You want me to do what?" Robert asked.

"The issue is that she has already created problems, serious problems: One is the money—and that's a considerable one. The other is that we have spent our lives building what she could destroy with a stroke of whimsy, vindictiveness or misplaced idealism. We were wrong about her; she lacks vision and doesn't understand the importance of our mission. She does not share our ideals and goals. And she's no kid. When she's sober, she knows exactly what she's doing. We valued her for good reason. But if we don't recover the records and her private notes, there's no telling what could happen. You must understand that," Carmen said.

Robert demurred. "Sophie's straight now, Carmen. I know for a fact that she's been clean for months. She'll come around and return the money. She was high when she took it, and she got frightened. As far as the records are concerned, she probably burnt them or threw them into the Thames. You can't fault her for the problems we have within the organization. Most of them we created ourselves and she hasn't told anyone. She would never do that."

"No one has the right to make these types of decisions on their own, Robert. And I reiterate, it matters little whether I agree or disagree with you. Our course of action has already been decided and nothing you can say or do will change that."

"What are you suggesting?" Robert asked.

"You must tell us where she is." The cardinal's tone was authoritative, his face red.

"I thought you'd say that. What if I don't know where she is?"

"Lying would be a very poor choice for you to make. You are a student of history, are you not, Robert? You know what happens when people defy the will of God. You must make the right choice. And you must consider the alternatives."

"Choice? What choice do I have?"

Carmen stepped closer to the young man who had brought him so many converts and helped set up the organization's financial empire. "I need your guarantee that you will recover the money Sophie has taken from us and see to it that she cannot do us any more harm. Can you do this?" He searched Robert's eyes for evidence that he could.

Robert paused. His left foot pushed a rock around on the gravel. He answered, "Yes."

"Good. Then make the necessary arrangements and keep me informed of your progress. I want to know your every move."

"How long do I have?"

"Three weeks. If we don't call the Vatican by then and tell them everything has been taken care of, they will use their own people. And then you yourself will have some problems."

The Cardinal put his arm around Robert and began leading him out of the square. He was still unconvinced that this was the best course of action. Robert's commitment to the cause was wavering and he would have to be watched closely.

The sun was gaining momentum on the clouds as they reached the motionless man beside the empty wine bottle. As they walked by, Robert made a slight gesture, and the derelict came to life. Leaping to his feet, he caught the cardinal in a stranglehold.

"I'm sorry, Carmen," Robert said, "but like you said, things have gotten way out of control."

A black car emerged from the northwest corner of the square and screeched to a stop beside them. Within seconds, the eminent Cardinal Carmen Hernandez had been forced inside and the car disappeared in the direction of a small airport on the city's outskirts.

In the back seat, Robert was pondering what they all had done—the illegal banking maneuvers, the incredible amounts of money stolen from depositors, the bogus loans, the movements of the money to church shell companies, the payoffs, and the absence of regulatory investigations. Then he thought about Sophie, her activities before she'd left for the U.S., her recent turnaround, and the money she'd taken.

The car veered to avoid a roadway construction site and Robert was slammed against the right side door. As a wave of terror struck him, he thought their plan had been compromised. But the driver quickly regained control and they continued on, losing no time. Trying to quiet himself, Robert vowed to himself that once he got to Sophie, he would clear his conscience and tell her everything he had done to help the cardinal and those in Rome build the Opus Dei organization. He knew she would believe him, forgive him. She trusted him. To make sure of it, he was bringing her an offering—the not-so-holy Cardinal Carmen Hernandez, the corrupt priest who had abused and confused her. The *kidnapped Cardinal who was grunting like a pig at his feet.*

TWELVE

**Madrid, Spain
October 15**

The Opus Dei Small Rectory in Spain

The phone rang loudly in Bishop Juan Carlos Ruiz's office near the Monasterio de la Encarnacion in Madrid. It did so eight times before the aging follower of Josemaria Escriva de Balaguer, preoccupied in searching his desk for records he thought might have been copied, finally took the time to answer it.

"What do you mean, Hernandez is missing?" The fat, balding churchman came to attention. "What's going on?"

"*Your officer* has not yet informed you?" the caller asked. "Cardinals seem to have disappeared."

"Maybe they are simply late for services related to the *Conclave*," Ruiz stated, "Missing Cardinals. How is it possible?"

"One didn't show up for a funeral service he was scheduled to attend, Your Eminence," the caller said, choosing his words carefully. "The last time he was seen was yesterday morning, leaving the chancery, around 5 a.m."

"Where was he going?" Juan Carlos was listening to the caller's every word.

"He told his housekeeper he had a meeting with someone and would be gone only a few hours."

"Why didn't you call me sooner?" The bishop was annoyed with the young priest who managed the cardinal's office.

"We had to rule out any compromising situations before we could list him as being abducted, Your Eminence. We did not want to alarm you."

"I understand. What leads do you have? Where did he go? Who was he with?"

"We do have a few, Your Eminence. Cardinal Hernandez took a car from the chancery garage and drove to Trafalgar Square. We think he met with just one man and we believe it was someone he knew. The car has been recovered."

"Who did he meet with?"

"We are not certain. But someone else is gone from London."

"Don't play games with me! Who is it?"

"Robert Hathaway."

"That son of a bitch," he muttered. "He wants to trade. Have you checked the airports and the trains?"

"We are doing that now, Your Eminence." The caller waited patiently for further instructions.

"I want to be kept informed about every development. Do you hear me?"

"Yes, your Eminence."

Juan Carlos slammed down the phone. Carmen Hernandez was his closest ally and in all likelihood he was now in the hands of a protégé who showed strong signs of becoming unmanageable.

Quickly considering his next move, he picked up the phone and dialed the number that would connect him to the private office at the Vatican. Bishop Zagranski had to be informed of the abduction and it was imperative that a meeting of all the principal Opus Dei officers be arranged immediately.

THIRTEEN

Ontario
The Same Day

The priest is with Sophie at the
Convent and the Institute

Sophie and Julien walked through the gates of the convent unaware of the kidnapping of Cardinal Carmen Hernandez. They had skipped midday prayers to take a hike up into the mountains. Deep in conversation, they had climbed further than they intended to and after several hours of walking in circles, they realized they were lost. Thankfully, with darkness came the dim lights of the convent and they had been able to follow them back.

Young Sister Denise rushed out when she saw them coming down the path. "Where have you been? We've been worried sick about you!"

Julien smiled at her affectionate concern. "We were in the hills. This woman loves to exercise and it was beautiful up there. We're sorry to have alarmed you, Sister Denise."

"Mother Superior is waiting for you. She's in her office with a man who is looking for Sophie."

"Robert!" Sophie uttered. "I knew he'd come!"

"No, Sophie, it's not your Robert. It's an older man, a man of the cloth."

Sophie's heart fluttered, wondering who had found her, fearing the worst.

"What does he look like, Denise?" Julien asked, sensing Sophie's alarm.

"Old, worn, grey and disheveled. He seems anxious, very fidgety. He told Mother Superior that he's a friend of Sophie's."

"A friend of mine," Sophie said, trying to think of who might fit the description,

"*Mother Superior* has been with him since just after you two left. They've been talking for hours."

"About what?" Julien asked knowing that news traveled quickly within the convent's walls.

"It seems urgent. I think *it has something to do with Pope Paul VI and Monsignor Escriva*. One of the sisters heard the names mentioned a number of times. We think Mother Superior is worried—she called for tea four times."

They all went quietly to Julien's room, knowing it would take more than a meek-looking clergyman to upset the Mother Superior.

"What's he after?" Sophie asked. She was getting herself ready for flight.

"We couldn't hear much more, only that he has something that he wants to discuss with you."

"What?"

"I have no idea."

Julien pulled her warm-up coat over her head and threw it on the bed. Walking over to her closet she took out an old tennis racket and held it out as if she intended to use it as a weapon. She then motioned for the other two women to follow her.

"Let's see what the little man wants, Sophie, and why he's had such an effect on our good Mother Superior," Julien said, leading the way from her room.

Father Timothy, sitting in a straight-back chair in the middle of the plain room, didn't move a muscle when the three young women came into the Mother Superior's office. The first thing he noticed was how different Sophie looked from when he'd seen her last. A surge of warm feelings rushed through him.

Sophie was astonished to find that the visitor was the old priest. "Father Timothy, *what are you doing here?*"

"I have come *to share something with you, my child,*" he said somberly, grateful for the obvious strength the good sisters' healing had brought her.

"Who is he?" Julien asked, glancing around the room, still alert.

"*He's the priest from the Institute.* The one I told you about."

"A priest you meet at a convent, lived with at an Institute... wants to *share... a secret with you*?" Julien asked.

Mother Superior, sensing Julien's concern, got up with some difficulty from her rickety chair and walked around the desk to stand between her and Father Timothy and motioned for Julien to sit down. "Father Timothy has brought us word of something rather startling. It seems to involve us all."

Julian lowered herself onto the worn blue couch, her eyes never straying from the priest. There was something spooky about him and she didn't trust the situation.

Sophie turned and after clumsily tripping over a footstool sat down next to Julian. Once settled, she looked at the old priest with compassion, *remembering the conversations they'd had about life and death*, and the drug experiences that had almost killed them both. The turmoil and pain she'd seen in him were still present and again she wondered what was eating at him. "Why have you come here, Father Timothy? How did you find me?"

He spoke slowly, in a tone that touched everyone. "God has sent me, child, to tell you about something that is of tremendous value. It is a *rare treasure* which was given to us many years ago, by a great man of the church." The old man's eyes gleamed.

He rose slowly and laid his shriveled hand on her shoulder. *"It is time, my child, for you to begin your journey with us.* I have come a long way to find you." Julien studied him, still trying to decide whether or not he was dangerous. Sophie, thinking that the hospital hadn't cured him of the belief that he had been chosen to do something incredible, shifted her feet uncomfortably.

Again it was the old nun who directed them. "I, too, was startled by the arrival of Father Timothy," she said calmly. "I was especially troubled after he told me why he'd come. Like you, I wondered about the truth of what he is saying. But, he has the holes in his hands and feet and the wound on his side, *the stigmata of Christ*. He says that it first began when Pope Paul VI came to the church in Galilee. Realizing this, I think a full explanation of everything is in order. Perhaps you should start from the beginning Father Timothy, wherever that is. Once you have convinced us that you're indeed not crazy, we will call this Father Rovarik, who you say can help us."

FOURTEEN

New England
October 16

*Silas searches after the secret for
the head of the brotherhood*

The Gypsy priest from the Church of the Multiplication had led Silas Willoughby down one blind alley after another in his search for *the missing relic*. He had kept him busy for weeks. After having visited too much of the Middle East, Silas now believed that an aging Benedictine priest whose name was Timothy Childs had the relic somewhere in the United States and that Rovarik knew where.

His search now took him to New England. Driving north on Interstate 91, he decided that Rovarik was involved with the new faction in the church that was opposing the interests of the Opus Dei. He wondered how much his employers knew about their activities.

As he pondered these things, heavy rain began to splash against the windshield of his car and he could barely see the road in front of him. He wondered how was it that these people knew things the Opus Dei didn't know. There was no doubt in his mind that that they had been given the cloth. He believed that his superiors were correct in assuming that Pope Paul VI had brought it to them. Not liking the developments in Rome that were garnering extraordinary power for Escriva and his followers, Pope Paul VI had apparently decided to subvert them and involved Leigh Rovarik, Timothy Childs and others in doing so.

Silas's thoughts returned to the Church of the Holy Sepulcher in Jerusalem and the powers he had felt there that disturbed and frightened him. He shivered, thinking about it. He loathed these feelings. In his profession, fear and uncertainty usually meant death.

FIFTEEN

London
The Same Day

***The brotherhood is trying to find
the kidnapped cardinal***

Chapel music could not entirely mask the screaming inside Ashwell House as the young woman struggled to free herself from the rope bindings. The Pembridge Square mansion, home to several high-ranking Opus Dei ministers and lay persons, had routinely hosted Monsignor Escriva on business trips and was often used as an administrative annex. But today, it was the site of an unofficial interrogation.

The wails from the second-floor *confessional room* were *louder than usual. Although similar cleansing rituals had been held in honor of Monsignor Escriva* for *decades all over the world tonights was much more brutal*. The inquisitors weren't confining themselves to just listening to sins. They were trying to find out where

The Brown Code

Robert Hathaway had taken Cardinal Hernandez. And there was a time factor to consider now.

An agitated young priest was the one questioning the woman. Between harsh strokes from *a whip*, he told her that her soul would be damned to Hell forever unless she revealed the information he wanted. Three other priests with him had spent the last hour with her and were preparing themselves to step up the intensity of the inquiry. The girl had been persistent, answering every question in the same manner, but they, too, were obstinate. Now she was faltering and, being reasonably certain that someone must have helped Robert, they were not taking her "no" for an answer.

"Where have they taken him? Where are they now?" The priest's fingers *turned a metal screw that tightened a blade-studded garter belt, the cilice, around her thigh*. Her body shook violently as it was tensioned. Feebly, she told the priests one more time that she knew nothing. Blood and spit rimmed her mouth as she tried unsuccessfully to clear her rapidly closing airway. The vile liquids dribbled down her neck as she coughed feebly and began convulsing. She was trying desperately to hold on when her head was slammed backwards from a violent tug, followed by a forceful blow from a fist to her head. What little was left of her vision faded completely.

"You are losing your battle with us, girly. And the price you'll pay for your lies will be a penance worse than death." Bishop Juan Carlos Ruiz, the oldest of the inquisitors, was now standing directly in front of her. The beady-eyed priest knew he couldn't go to Rome without some answers. "Where are they, you lying little bitch?"

Her gaze held his soul for a brief second as she said slowly, murmuring each word with difficulty, "May God *forgive you* for what you are doing." Trying to cloak herself in her forgiveness of those who tortured her, she drifted silently into the peace and safety of her own soul.

Her words made Juan Carlos Ruiz doubt himself and the cause, but only for a moment, before he returned to his mission with renewed zeal. Again, he slammed at her brutally with his closed hand. It was as if everything he had been taught as a consecrated priest of Jesus Christ had been forgotten entirely. Looking at the unconscious girl, and then at the other two women lying in the corner of the room, he angrily turned to one of the other priests. "Bring in two more. Perhaps the next few won't be so fucking committed."

While the Opus Dei priests were trying to find out where the kidnapped Cardinal was taken to and what happened to the secret, in the next room of the brownstone residence hall another member of the brotherhood was having a repentance experience.

Silas had been tricked. The brothers had lied, choosing death instead of revealing the true secret. Silas didn't have the strength to call *his patron*, the Secretary to the Pope. He planned on hiding at this Opus Dei house knowing the Secretary would protect him in the Opus Dei sanctuary.

After all, it had been the Secretary who gave Silas life in the first place...***in that small rectory in Spain***.

Kneeling on the wooden floor, Silas prayed for ***forgiveness***. Then, stripping off his robe, he reached again for the whip-like *Discipline*, to do a little self-inflicted torture of his own.

SIXTEEN

Martha's Vineyard, Massachusetts
October 19

Robert and Sophie go looking for 'the Key'
to the secret kept at the Knight's bank

Sophie was surprised to get the car onto the ferry so easily. But it was autumn, cold and gusty, and tourists were no longer as anxious to go over to Martha's Vineyard as they were in the summer.

Feeling tired and weak, Julien decided to stay in the car, opting for a nap. She didn't like being on the top side of boats anyway. So Sophie and Robert went up by themselves and were alone for the first time in months. After visiting the snack shop for coffee, they headed for the open deck to experience what Robert humorously called the wildness of the sea. Sophie privately thought that it was time to finally be together.

They wobbled out of the enclosure, still trying to get their sea legs, noticing that the Cape's winds were not blowing as ferociously as they'd anticipated. In a cozy spot just behind the wheel house, they sat down and embraced tenderly.

"Peaceful, isn't it? The island should be quiet now, with all the visitors gone," Sophie murmured. "I'm so glad to be with you. The last time I made this trip, I wasn't thinking very well. I remember spending most of the time throwing up and falling down. I'd needed a haven and Abby's house was the only safe place I could think of. She had no idea what was going on with me. I called her in a panic and she said I should come over and stay as long as I needed to. I think her housekeeper met me at the dock in Vineyard Haven."

"It's all too crazy, Sophie. None of it's worth it," Robert said. "Let's stop the whole thing and just go away." He looked at her, wanting to feel that they could.

"Let's leave and keep going and never turn around." Sophie's voice was warm with affection.

"Yeah," he said, "This feels so good. I've missed you so much." He kissed her gently on the forehead, trying to quell all thoughts about the money and concentrate only on her. They looked out into the darkness, saying nothing more for minutes about their problems. Robert finally broke their silence. "So, where exactly is it that we're going?" he asked, wrapping his arms around her, hugging her tightly to him to protect her.

"I'm taking you to Abby's house and I'm going to keep you all to myself, forever and ever. No one will find us." Sophie said it so convincingly she almost believed it herself, until Robert shattered the mood.

"Be serious, Sophie!" he said, regretting his thoughts but unable to control them. "We're here to *get the bank records back*, not for a holiday. We can have that later, after we're through. Is everything at your aunt's?"

It was just his need to focus on the practical, she told herself. But the way he asked her the question was tainted. She broke free. "You're only interested in what I have, Robert, aren't you? Christ, nothing's changed. I still don't know who you are."

"Get hold of yourself, Sophie," he said in the paternal tone she had once loved but no longer did. "This is serious. No more little-girl games. These bastards don't want us around anymore and maybe this just isn't the time for love. I think we'd better concern ourselves with staying alive. Or maybe you don't care about that anymore."

Sophie felt sick. This was not someone she wanted to be with. She got up and just about ran across the deck to get away from him. Bitterly, she remembered the last time she'd been on this ferry. It seemed to be a world-and-a-half away now. She'd been drunk, lonely and frightened, and the only thing she'd wished for was to be with Robert. But now that he was here, she didn't want to be near him. In less than a minute she reached the car. She pounded on the hood to wake Julien up.

"What's the... matter with you?" Half-asleep, Julien unlocked the door.

"He doesn't understand, Julien. He'll never understand. Why don't I ever learn?"

"Understand what? What did you tell him? Did you tell him about the *tapes*?" Julien was struggling to be alert.

"No. What he doesn't understand is that I don't give a damn about the money or the priests from hell who wants it. I don't care about that anymore. And he does."

"I don't get it. Maybe my synapses are firing slowly, but what are you talking about?"

Julien could see Robert approaching them, a concerned look on his face.

"Sometimes you just have enough of this bullshit, Julien, especially the money stuff. You just want someone to love you for who you are and forget about all that crap."

"OK, calm down. We'll talk all about it when we get to the house," Julien said, folding Sophie up in her arms, trying to help her settle down.

The door opened and Robert climbed in beside them. It was obvious that they'd been talking about him. Looking to Julien for support, he said, "I'm sorry, Sophie. I wasn't thinking. I know I'm not giving you what you need. But I'm only trying to help keep us alive. Maybe love will just have to wait until we get out of this." His message of embarrassment and remorse was almost palpable.

"Speak for yourself, Robert," Julien said, thinking about how much she cared for the woman who was crying in her arms.

Robert turned his most sincere look on and his eyes moved softly over them both. Wordlessly, he asked if he could lean his head on Sophie's shoulder and then did so without her permission. Sophie had a right to be furious with him. But her anger wasn't going to be of much help. They were all in this together and they would have to be sharp if any of them was going to get out alive.

They were all quite tired by the time they arrived at their destination in Edgartown. Abby's house, an 18th-century sea captain's mansion, was identified by a highly polished brass plaque on the front door as The Captain Warren Jessop House. It was set off by itself, at the end of South Water Street, on a series of shallow cliffs. White with black shutters and a grey slate roof, it was obviously in the process of being painted and repaired. There were ladders and paint buckets strewn all over the driveway and the front lawn.

Sophie showed her friends to the guest rooms and then gave them a brief tour, pointing out family pictures and priceless antiques. For Robert, the exquisite furnishings were the most interesting. In his mind, having access to places like this, her inheritance, and her social position were a strong part of Sophie's allure. Sophie and Julien, however, thought nothing of the valuables. For them, the house and its contents were meaningless; Abby's home was just a lovely place to be.

SEVENTEEN

October 20

'The Key' is a 'Right Eyeball'

It was neither the screeching sea gulls from the docks below nor the whistling wind at the unlatched door leading up to the widow's walk that stirred Julien. What woke her was the dull pain in the back of her head that had become a fundamental part of her life in the past few weeks. It made sleeping soundly for anything more than a few hours impossible and the reality of death even more real. Again, she was greeting a day before she was ready to. After saying morning prayers and taking her medications, she went downstairs to see if anyone was up.

Sophie and Robert were already in the day room drinking coffee, talking quietly, watching the fog lift itself off the harbor. "Good morning, Julien," Sophie said, gentle in her greeting, knowing how painful Julien's mornings were.

"The same to the both of you!" Julien kissed Sophie, met Robert's look with a smile, and sat down. She stroked the smooth cherry wood of the table appreciatively.

"Sophie told me about your condition, Julien." Robert poured out a cup of coffee and placed it before her thoughtfully. Despite his jealousy over their closeness, and knowing that she was nearing death, he almost liked her. Maybe everything would work out, despite Sophie's naive idealism. He moved closer to Sophie and began massaging her neck.

"It's put life into perspective for me. Some things just don't seem as urgent as they used to be. I guess my focus has changed a lot. But let's not dwell on my affliction, let's get on with things. What have you two been talking about besides me and my problems? You're not still fussing, I hope." Julien looked at Sophie, who seemed to be in love with Robert again.

"Sophie was telling me why she came here the last time, Julien."

Sophie returned Julien's raised brow with an expression of her own, then picked up on the conversation. "When I was young, I came here a lot to visit my Aunt Abby. We spent many of our school vacations on the Vineyard. Abby was the only one who seemed to find time for us kids—everyone else was too busy doing important business things. When I started losing it, I had the good sense to call her. I tracked her down in China and she told me to come here. She said there would be people here to help me. I don't know what I would have done without her."

Sophie drank some of her coffee and put English muffins in the toaster before going on. "Abby came here to get away from the nonsense herself. She leaves the island mostly to do research now—she's an author. She's been much more than an aunt to me. More like an older sister. And she has good friends here on the Vineyard.

When they heard I was in trouble, half crazy, a few of them came over to check on me. I guess it was obvious that I needed more help than they could give me, so someone took me up to Brattleboro. The rest of the story you both know." Sophie shrugged.

"Why did you bring the records here? It's an easy trail. Anyone could have followed you," Robert said, unable to stop himself from pressuring her.

"I didn't bring anything with me when I came."

"You didn't?" He scowled.

"No. I mean, the records weren't with me. Parts of them were already hidden here."

Julien tried to change the subject. "Who wants muffins?" she said. "How about some butter and jam?" She opened the refrigerator. "There's sweet butter and cranberry jam in here."

"I was actually coherent enough," Sophie continued, "to know that no one realized what I'd done yet and that besides the banks, I alone had the numbers of the new accounts that I set up. I didn't want to chance taking them with me on the plane so I sent them over here before I left."

"To your aunt?" Robert asked.

"No, to an old friend, Buddy." She winked at Julien, who was smiling at her, and leaned back in her chair, thinking about how best to continue. She decided the best course of action was to show them, as she had planned. Picking up her coat from one of the kitchen chairs she walked in the direction of the front door, beckoning for them to follow her.

"Come on you two. The weather's beautiful outside and I want to take you somewhere. It's time to go catch *the brass ring*."

The Flying Horses Carousel in Oak Bluffs is billed as the oldest operating merry-go-round in the United States. It is world-renowned for the beauty and craftsmanship of its horses, especially their lifelike expressions, elaborate coloring, and their manes and tails of natural horsehair.

On the way there, Sophie told her friends about the famous carousel. "My aunt has been involved in the Flying Horses restoration project ever since she first came here in the '70s. She used to bring us here when we were little girls. I'll never forget the first time I saw the chipped horse with the reddish mane. For me, it was love at first sight. All the horses have names etched on them now but they didn't back then. So I gave him one. I called him Buddy and every time I came back, the first thing I wanted to do was to go see Buddy."

"We're going for a ride on a merry-go-round?" Robert asked, impatient once again.

"Calm down, Robert. No, we're not going to ride the merry-go-round. We're going to see Buddy. He's waiting for us."

It was only a 10-minute drive from Edgartown to the Victorian town of Oak Bluffs, where Sophie led them to an octagonal red-and-white building and walked all around it. Being reasonably certain that no maintenance or repair work was going on, she began to work the lock on one of the side doors.

Not knowing exactly what to do, Robert and Julien surveyed the empty streets. "What are you doing?" Julien asked.

"I'm breaking in. Isn't that obvious?" Sophie answered.

"Do you think that's a good idea?" Robert asked.

"The records are in there," Sophie responded. "Here, I need help with this, Robert."

"Jesus Christ, Sophie, this is breaking and entering. Don't we have enough problems already?" Robert had noticed the police station around the corner on the way in.

"Just get me inside. We're wasting time talking about it."

Robert took a last look around, then forced the hasp and lock apart with a rusty bar he found under the stairs. The plate sprung away and the doors opened with a loud clang. After they slipped into the cold, dark building, he fastened the broken doors loosely with a discarded piece of rope, hoping they would stay shut.

About 15 feet away, barely visible, was the merry-go-round, its horses covered with sheets and dirty blankets, dust clinging to their exposed legs. Sophie shined a flashlight she had brought on each horse until she located her Buddy. "Hello, old friend. Have you missed me? I've missed you." Taking off his covers, she stroked his mane lovingly and rested her face on his crimson bridle.

"We're not safe in here," Robert warned.

Turning on a ceiling light, Sophie said, "This won't take long." Looking tenderly at her favorite horse she continued. "Thank you for helping me, Buddy. I knew you would."

Robert was glancing from one exit to the other, thinking about the racket they'd made getting in. He cringed when Sophie walked over to a workbench and started pushing around an assortment of tools until she found a screwdriver.

Walking back, she again talked to the horse as if he were alive. "Don't worry, Buddy. We'll fix you up and make you beautiful again as soon as we can."

She inserted the tip of the screwdriver into the corner of Buddy's '*right eye socket*' and forced a clear sulfide sphere out, catching it as it fell. Then she sympathetically patted his face again, feeling terrible.

When she turned to her friends, she held the object in the palm of her hand for them to see. "Let's get out of here," she said. She pulled hard on the string of the light and walked quickly past them. Stumbling over a ladder, she momentarily lost her balance. She headed blindly for the doors. Her only thought was to get out as fast as she could and to hide her tears. She hated herself for having mutilated her beloved, magical horse.

Robert, Julien and Sophie returned to Edgartown by a back road through the town of Chilmark. Robert assumed that they had at least part of what everyone was looking for and took note of the fact that if this was true, they were all targets now.

Once they had settled back in at Abby's house, Sophie began to explain the significance of the glass eye that she had donated to the restoration project. "Not long after I moved into my new apartment and assumed my responsibilities at the Dawliffe Educational Foundation, I became aware of certain problems that existed with certain banks. Have either of you ever heard of the *London Boys?"* Sophie smiled, knowing that at least one of them knew who they were.

"Don't you mean the Chicago Boys?" Robert said innocently.

"No. The London Boys. Same species, different group. It's my own label." She hesitated dramatically, then continued. "It all began late one night when Carmen was with me in my apartment. A man found his way up to us, a small, timid kind of fellow. He said it was important that Carmen talk to him about some mutual friends they had. It was unlike Carmen to waste time on someone like that, but he did. This guy said that one of the men he was talking about was Leonardo Roberto Calvi, a man who Carmen had done a lot of business with years before."

"I remember reading about that. Wasn't he the guy from the bank fraud scandal? The one found hanging in the museum near Blackfriars Bridge in London?" Julien interrupted her. "It was in all the newspapers, the Banco Ambrosiano affair. I think it was about 1982."

Knowing it was and concerned at the direction Sophie's conversation had already taken, Robert said nothing.

"Yes," Sophie answered her. "His death was described in the tabloids as a suicide," she said. Her eyes rolled. "It seemed that Carmen's visitor knew a great deal about the activities of Leonardo Roberto Calvi, especially around the time of his death. He knew, for instance, that Calvi had been with Carmen and some other Opus Dei people the week before he died. He told us that he could implicate some of them in many illegitimate financial deals that had taken place with Calvi. He suggested that Carmen speak to him privately about it."

"He didn't elaborate in front of you?" Julien asked.

"No. He asked Carmen to meet him somewhere else, at a neutral place."

"Then what happened?" Julien was listening to every word and Robert was slowly becoming afraid.

"Carmen gave him his private number and told him to call him the following day. The man left as silently as he arrived." It was the fear on his face and the way his body shook when he talked to Carmen that Sophie remembered the most. "Carmen told me not to say anything to anyone. He said the guy could be a misguided zealot or a dangerous creep, that I should forget the whole incident. He promised that he would take care of it. But he was very agitated."

"How so?" Julien asked.

"Something the little man said really rattled him. The first thing Carmen did after he left was to go into the other room and call the Vatican. It was the first time he'd ever done this kind of thing when we were together, so it must have been urgent. He was very good at separating work and play, and always said that nothing was more important to him than our prayerful devotions." Sophie looked away from Robert.

"What exactly was going on, Sophie?" He couldn't help himself from wanting to know the details about her relationship with Hernandez, the one that had been eating at him for so long now.

She skillfully avoided his question. "About a week later, Carmen came over and asked me for my help. He said he'd met with the man and that he did have information about some investments made by Calvi and other Opus Dei people that involved the Vatican."

Julien *took the eye* from her and began to play with it herself. "Yeah, and then?" she said encouragingly.

"Carmen asked me to come to the next meeting to help him analyze what he was offering. He said he didn't trust anyone but me to be there."

"You found the links between the Vatican and the bankrupted banks?" Robert was running way ahead of her.

"Not at first. The man was very careful about what he told us. It took us weeks to get him to talk about how the money had been moved into the Vatican's banks by the London Boys. They were unscrupulous bastards and very cautious about covering their asses. The sums they stole were phenomenal."

"But the Vatican repaid the Banco Ambrosiano depositors almost $250 million dollars in 1985, Sophie," Robert corrected her. Julien made a mental note of how broad Robert's knowledge was. "I was already working at Opus Dei headquarters. We contributed heavily to the settlement monies because the Vatican didn't have enough available cash at the time. You know how hard it was for the church in the 1970's, Sophie. It was in serious financial trouble. *Pope John Paul even acknowledged it publicly. Without the financial support of the Opus Dei, the Catholic Church would have been broke."*

"That's true Robert, but it was nothing compared to what the Vatican got out. And why are you trying to protect the priests? Even now!"

"All right. I know some of the story, Sophie, but I don't think I know what you know," he said, not responding directly to her question. "Please don't be upset with me." He did his best to look sincere, not wanting to agitate her again.

"Ah, excuse me, you guys. If you could stop bickering, I would really appreciate an explanation of what you're talking about," Julien broke in.

"Whose turn is it?"

"Ladies first."

"Thank you. Well, Julien, it's like this. They've stolen a lot of money, many billions of dollars. The London Boys, the Opus Dei, the Vatican, they all worked together in this.

Our little informant, who we nicknamed the Venetian, proved to us beyond a reasonable doubt that many large transfers of money were made into the Vatican's banks from a number of the London Boys' banks in Europe and the U.S. before they failed. The monies were channeled through several Opus Dei foundation accounts in London. The sums Robert spoke of that were paid back were a drop in the bucket compared to the actual sums they got out from all of them."

Sophie was preparing herself to tell them more. She took the horse's eye back and held it to the light so Julien and Robert could see the tiny objects which were inside.

"Christ, those banks operated all over the world. How were you able to piece it all together?" Robert was curious and more than a little concerned.

"The Venetian was a frightened man, Robert, but he wasn't stupid. Actually, he was quite clever. And all the bankers had kept excellent private records of their transactions. Anyway, as time went on, we learned that in addition to being close to Leonardo Roberto Calvi the Venetian was also friendly with Michele Sindona, the banker who was jailed in the U.S. because of his involvement in the Franklin National Bank scandal. Sindona is probably more well known in Europe because of the collapse of his bank, the Banca Privata Finanziaria, and its relationship with the IOR. He's dead now, too."

"What's the IOR?" Julien asked.

"*The Institute for the Works of Religion.* It's an investment bank directly affiliated with *the Vatican Bank.* The IOR invests heavily in high-risk markets and makes a lot of money," Robert broke in.

Sophie gave the eyeball to him and started pacing around the room. She wasn't at all comfortable with his train of thought. "It hasn't always made money, Robert. *There have been some real bad years and they have made some horrible investments.*"

"That was in the early '80s, Sophie. The bank's management was changed and the problems were eliminated."

"Yeah. Eliminated like Calvi and Sindona were, hung or poisoned in jail. We both know how some of the problems were dealt with, don't we." Again, Robert seemed to be defending the wrong people.

"Hey, don't get me wrong, I'm not making excuses for them."

"Good, don't." Ignoring his comments, she went on. "So we have these meetings taking place in a safe place, Julien. There's the cardinal, the Venetian, and little ol' me in this suite at the Park Lane Hotel in Westminster, and we're discussing the illegal 'donations' made to the church by all of the London Boys' banks. Quite matter-of-factly the Venetian informs us that all of the money transfers promised to the priests back then were not made. He informs us that an assortment of securities and other valuables which were removed from the failed banks are still waiting in the wings, so to speak."

"He says," she continued, "that he will hand over the convertibles to us if certain problems are taken care of for him, including his need for protection. He tells the cardinal that he is not at all comfortable with some of the people who are associated with the Vatican and the IOR. That some of his friends are now dead because they trusted them."

"Back up, Sophie. I thought you said the IOR was an investment bank affiliated with the Vatican Bank. So what's the connection between the banks and the IOR?"

Robert peered into the horse's eye at a little cat figure. He was smiling because he knew many of the answers.

"Do you know who Archbishop Manuel Zagranski is, Julien?" Sophie asked. She glanced sideways at Robert, looking for another wisecrack to be made. None came.

"Yes, the first secretary to Pope John Paul II."

"That's correct, and he was a very close friend of Monsignor Escriva. Escriva, in fact, was his benefactor and Zagranski has succeeded him as the head of the Opus Dei organization. He's been in charge of it for the last 15 years. He's also been the director of the IOR for the last 13 years."

"And?"

"And he was a good friend of both Calvi and Sindona. Back in the 1980s, the London Boys did a lot of business with Zagranski. Then there's the little matter of the Rumasa scandal."

Julien was clearly having trouble keeping the names of the bankers straight. Noticing her difficulty, Sophie slowed her pace down a notch. "Another banking organization, Julien. You don't need to know all of the details. The point is that these guys were everywhere. The Rumasa organization was a business consortium which owned about 20 banks and hundreds of other businesses all over Europe. It went belly up in 1983." She paused a moment for Julien to take it all in.

"The head of the Rumasa was a man by the name of Josemaria Ruiz-Mateos. And guess what? Ruiz-Mateos arranged bogus loans to be made from a half-dozen of his banks to the IOR just before they went under.

This illegal business was approved by Archbishop Zagranski himself. The monies all of the bankers loaned to the IOR, in other words the Vatican, were quite substantial. If you add up the totals, the sums are billions of dollars."

"So the church borrowed money from some banks that eventually failed. That's it? And the bankers knew each other?" Julien directed her question to Robert, whose knee was bouncing up and down under the table.

Sophie didn't give him a chance to answer her.

"Sweetheart, it's not just the money itself, but where it came from. And it's why so many 'unsecured loans'—or whatever you want to call them—were ever made in the first place. It's also about where the money is now. You must understand that most of it has never been repaid to anyone. It's been free money, so to speak. And the IOR, Rumasa, the Banco Ambrosiano, and the other banks are not the only banks involved in this scheme. People don't realize how incredibly profitable bank failures were in the 1980s. It's quite a quagmire." Sophie sighed.

"You're saying that the church got all this money in the forms of loans. Why would it want to borrow so much money?"

Sophie appreciated her friend's naive confusion. "Good Lord, Julien!" she said. "They wanted it because it was there to be had. They had money problems. Cathedrals, properties and icons are fine on paper, but its liquid assets were pitiful. Lack of cash can be a critical problem in any business and selling off St. Peter's wasn't acceptable. Overtly anyway."

"She's right, Julien—the church is, after all, just a business." Robert broke in. "You can do more good for people if you have money than if you don't. Even the church needs cash to operate. Don't you remember the financial problems in the church at the beginning of the century?"

"No."

"They were so broke after Pope Benedict XV died, in 1914, that they couldn't bring everyone in for a conclave to elect the new pope. The Cardinal Secretary of State had to borrow money to get everyone to Rome."

"And?" Julien prompted.

"*And in the 1980s, the need to protect its financial interests again became a primary concern for the Vatican.*" Sophie took the conversation back from Robert, changing its course.

"The Opus Dei is strong only if its doctrines and philosophies become an accepted part of the church's doctrines. This will be formally accomplished when Escriva is finally canonized. With it comes public recognition of his controversial teachings. Pope John Paul, of course, has heard a lot of stories about Escriva, both good and bad. Even among his faithful followers there is talk of him having being a very disturbed man. In the end though, the pope will do what's best financially for the church." Sophie waited again for Robert to say something but he didn't disagree with her this time.

"You see, Julien, the way for Manuel Zagranski to make sure the Opus Dei will be politically solvent is to solidify its financial control over the Vatican. The way to do that is by providing the church with the cash it needs to operate."

Sophie went to the refrigerator, took out a bottle, and poured sodas. Setting them on the table, she said, "It went something like this, Julien. With Calvi, Sindona and Ruiz-Mateos in his pocket, it was easy for Zagranski to get the funds he needed to solve the church's short-term cash flow problems. As the director of the IOR, he was in control of the church's money. He decided where it would come from and where it would go. In doing so, he set the agendas of the church. By the end of the 1980s, he was, for all intents and purposes, in charge of the politics of the entire church. The Opus Dei, with him at the helm, had succeeded in reaching some of its long-term objectives. They had seized control of many of the assets of the Roman Catholic Church."

Julien had one last question. "Why do you call them the London Boys?"

"Because being good little Opus Dei 'boys' they did most of their business in London, where Opus Dei's headquarters are. All the illegal money was channeled through the Opus Dei banks and the charities there," Sophie answered. Robert just nodded in agreement.

Pretending to be finished with her explanations, she collected the glasses and washed them. "Hey, you guys," she said when she was finished, "how about some music to change the atmosphere?" She turned on a portable radio, tuned in a station, and began to dance around the room. After the song was over she returned her attention to their conversation.

"But there was a little snag, Julien," she said, tapping a rhythm on the table. "The Venetian! They hadn't anticipated his arrival. They thought their people had eliminated all the variables, like Robert said, and that everything was under control. But it wasn't." Turning off the radio, she sat back down. "They knew nothing about the little man who came to see us. The timid man who sat nervously with us day after day had the means to topple the entire Opus Dei organization if he wanted to. And they didn't even know his name."

"Incredible!" was all Julien could think of to say.

Robert sat quietly, pretending to be amused. "How were the rest of the monies arranged?" he finally asked.

"The initial money was given to the IOR with no guarantees. You know that, Robert. Julien, dear, you really can't ask for collateral on stolen money, can you? But once it started flowing out from their banks to the Opus Dei foundations and then to the IOR, the bankers held back some of the securities and gave them to our little friend for safekeeping. With the money it got, the IOR set up small out-of-the-way banks and investment companies, mostly offshore, which invested heavily in some legitimate and some not-so-legitimate businesses, mostly communications companies in Central and South America and the Caribbean. Opus Dei is politically strong in Latin America so it was easy for them to stash money there. Apparently, all the companies they invested in have Opus Dei people managing them."

Playing with them, Sophie held a dish cloth in front of her face so that Robert and Julien could only see her eyes. She was not telling them everything she had learned from the Venetian.

Julien picked up the conversational thread Sophie left dangling. "So you have the London Boys gathering up buckets of money from banks that failed and routing the money into the Opus banks and then to the IOR which then sets up other lending institutions. These banks invest heavily in some companies in Latin America and elsewhere? The new banks are effectively operated by Zagranski and his Opus Dei people. Nice game." Although her training was in tennis, not business or finance, Julien was getting the picture.

"Precisely." Sophie was well aware of her friend's keen intellect.

"Everything seems to be going along smoothly—and then this little guy shows up to fuck things up." Sophie recalled the first time the Venetian told her and Carmen about how the London Boys protected themselves.

"At one time he was apparently an influential banker in Europe himself, one of the masterminds who put the whole bank failure scheme together in the first place. He became the London Boys' fail-safe mechanism in case anything went wrong. Something did go wrong. Everything. When Calvi was found hanging, the rest of the boys knew it was all over. When Sindona was found dead in the Italian prison and Ruiz-Mateos lost his mind waiting for them to come to kill him, the Venetian thought it best to get lost for awhile. He came to see Carmen only days after he came out of hiding."

"How exactly did they cover their asses, Sophie?" Robert asked.

"You mean, besides keeping duplicate copies of all the bank transfers their banks made to the church?"

"Yeah, besides that!" Robert couldn't help but grimace.

Sophie smirked, knowing she had him right where she wanted him, and directed her attention back to Julien. "The Vatican and its banks are not subject to outside banking laws, Julien. In other words, they're a world apart from the rest of us. The IOR, as a Vatican Bank affiliate, is therefore not subject to any bank inspections. Nor is it regulated by the Italian government. Any contributions made into it, its disbursements and investments—none of it is ever audited. Of course, that was a necessary ingredient in the plan. The Opus Dei foundations in London were able to launder the stolen securities because there were no regulators watching them either. And really, who would ever suspect the Catholic Church of being involved in a wild scheme like this!" Sophie took a second to catch her breath. "Money makes money, and everybody is happy except for the people whose life savings were deposited in the London Boys' banks. They lost everything."

Robert interrupted her. "The Venetian had the records with him in London?"

This time, Sophie didn't avoid his question. "No. He had most of it tucked safely away. The incriminating information he had was his ticket in and his bus fare out. That and a whole lot of stocks, bonds and some unholy precious metals that needed cleaning," Sophie didn't appreciate Robert's inquisitive tone of voice.

"What happened then?" He was staring into the horse's glass eye.

"It became apparent, as the weeks went on, that Carmen, being a loyal Opus Dei member, was operating under strict instructions from Manuel Zagranski to pull everything in without the knowledge of their old Sicilian friends, who because of their involvements in the first deals would still consider a significant amount of the money to be theirs. It was obvious that the Venetian knew this and was agreeable to do business with just the priests, if he got what he asked for. What he wanted was to sell off what he had and get out alive. He came to us thinking that if he took a little less, we would get rid of everything quietly without telling the bad guys what was going on."

"You cut a deal with him?" Robert felt himself getting closer to what he was after.

Sophie spoke slowly, not reacting to Robert's obvious impatience. "I told you that a lot of the securities stolen by the London Boys still needed to be laundered. But the Venetian was out of the banking business forever. None of what he had was any good to him unless it was washed."

"Yeah."

"Well, we just pushed it all through the Opus Dei foundation accounts in much the same way as it was done in the 1980s."

"And..."

"We bought it all. He agreed to take 25 percent for the lot of it and went away happy as a lark."

"Jesus Christ, Sophie. How much did you give him?"

"I'm not sure. I left quickly once all the first processes were initiated. Many, many millions of dollars were—are —involved. What the final amounts were though, I don't know for sure. We set it up so that he got his money at the same time the securities were presented to our banks."

"Jesus Christ, Sophie." Robert appeared shocked.

Sophie moved ahead. "Zagranski and his people bought their way into the store the first time around. But they had partners back then. This time, they didn't want to owe anyone anything. Zagranski really thought this would be his second big score—and if it had all worked out, the Opus Dei would have made the church cash solvent again and he would have secured his own position, maybe even be the next pope." The look on Julien's face told Sophie that she had to explain a bit more.

"It took us three weeks to set up the washes through the Opus Dei accounts. I used the banks of the Sacerdotal Society of the Holy Cross and the Dawliffe Educational Foundation to do it. I involved only the newer Opus Dei banks which were out of the country so that no one except our own people would know what was going on. When the washed funds came back in, I made the necessary arrangements for them to go off to the IOR."

Sophie took a deep breath. She looked at Julien, then at Robert, and decided to take the final plunge, even if it was being reckless. "But I didn't actually set it up so that the bulk of the money was sent to the IOR. I had a change of heart about halfway through. I arranged for a large portion of the cleaned money to be transferred out of the foundations' accounts into my own accounts." She looked at Robert again, hoping she was making the right decision in telling him all of this.

"How much is a large portion?" Julien asked.

"Like I said, Julien, I don't know what the final numbers were because I left as soon as I set everything in motion," Sophie said matter-of-factly.

"I don't believe it. Did Zagranski really think he'd get away with this? And what the hell were you thinking, Sophie?" Robert was amazed.

Sophie ignored his ranting and answered only the first part of his question. "Yes, I believe that Zagranski thought he would get away with it. But he's not all that bright. You know that, Robert. He's just insanely ambitious."

As she went on, Robert was trying to figure out how much she could have actually taken.

"OK," she said, "if you're trying to hide something these days, coding and locking computer files is too run-of-the-mill. Everyone is doing that sort of thing. It's boring. Sometimes it makes good sense not to be so obvious, to be creative by going backwards."

Smiling, she picked up the *glass sphere*. "If you look in the center of Buddy's eye you will see a number of lovely little objects that are in there. In between them, there is a tiny piece of microfilm positioned sideways so that it cannot be seen. Remember microfilm?"

Sophie *turned the eyeball from side to side* trying to find the small piece of film she had put there. She couldn't see it. "What they all did at the banks was quite ingenious, wasn't it, Robert? *But pay attention now, because I couldn't get everything on the film, just the account numbers at the banks where the money is now.* And I'm going to need your help to get it back."

EIGHTEEN

Tibet
October 21

An Old Woman at a Holy Shrine knows everything

The Gypsy woman listened to a bitter cold wind blowing through a cracked window in her room. The smell of her straw-stuffed bed permeated the chilly air and its dampness made her bones ache. Feeling the pain, she knew she would not be getting up today.

For hundreds of years, the monastery where she was had sheltered nuns, monks and other spiritual travelers looking for peace and the eternal truths. She was respected as being one of these seekers. Tight to her chest she hugged *a large glass ball* which was, like her, old, delicate and full of wisdom. It had last been her mother's, handed down from one member of her family to another, along with the ageless stories and teachings of the entire Gypsy race.

She peered into it carefully. Never again would she accept any of its false messages for truth as she had once done, she thought. She pondered why, years ago, she had so misread the signs in the glass and ignored her instinctive mistrust of what she saw there.

Looking away, she listened again to the sounds of the threatening currents and deeply breathed in the foul, musty air. The last time she had come here from her home near *Edinburgh, Scotland*, she had been so young, sent by the elders to look for the holy cloth they suspected was here. The monks had received her graciously and then, taking direction from their own signs and traditions, had entrusted their treasure to her.

Vividly, she remembered threading her way back down through the mountain passes, the relic carefully rolled into her pack. Anxiety returned to her as she remembered the descent and how the storms had attacked her and the porters as soon as they left the safety of the monastery. The disturbances, she had felt then, were nature's and God's warnings to her, but she had ignored them also.

Looking around the bare room, she shook her head and wondered at how muddled her thinking had been then. Lost in youthful indulgence, she had become part of a disturbed world. She had seen herself embarked upon the sacred journey that her mother and the elders had told her about ever since she was a child as they traveled with the carnivals through Europe. It was a mythological journey she was claiming. And she had been blinded by the exaltation. She clutched the globe like an old friend. It was all she had left. Her world—her mother, the elders, her friends—was gone and she was tired. And she had failed them all. For a moment she was able to erase some of the regret and picture herself as she had been at the time, pretty, vibrant and certain. But the delightful memory evaporated as soon as she moved slightly and felt the pain in her joints.

She sighed, looking down at her gnarled hands, swollen knuckles and tightly stretched skin.

In Rome, the priests had seemed so trustworthy. They had told her that the man called Escriva was a messenger sent by the Lord. How was she to have known what his motives were? She had not even considered that it was a mistake to trust him. Oh, how she understood it now. But her cherished crystal had been murky then, confusing.

Fortunately, she had seen the other signs and listened to companions who doubted the priest's motives before it was too late. In the end, it was another man of the cloth who had helped her. Pope Paul VI himself had come and wrested from Monsignor Escriva what was not his to have and misuse.

She chastised herself one last time before closing her eyes, sensing that her own end was near. It had been a long and arduous journey back up to the monastery and she knew she would never leave this place again. Humbly, she asked for God's forgiveness for her transgressions, especially in placing her trust in those who were false.

Her prayers were interrupted by *a young monk*. He bore a written message from *her brother*:

"The cloth has been located. Release your guilt and rest peacefully. Love, Leigh."

She drifted off, holding tightly to the crystal ball, the note, and her belief in man's absolute goodness. Her last thought was that she was not alone, neither in these remote mountains nor in her belief in the sanctity of life. It was comforting for her to know that others still believed, lived and worked to protect eternal truths and wisdom. Centuries ago, her ancestors had helped the holy one find His way to this holy place. One day, she thought, all that He had prophesied here would come to pass.

NINETEEN

☥

Rome
The Same Day

The Head of the Opus Dei and members meet at a Church property to talk about the Vatican's problems

The Vatican is situated in and around Saint Peter's Square in the northwestern section of Rome just west of the Tiber River. The square is surrounded by huge medieval walls with towering pillars and has six entrance gates. The most imposing structures are Saint Peter's Basilica, the world center for Roman Catholic worship, and the Palace of the Vatican, a complex of about 1,000 rooms, including those of the papal apartment and the central government offices of the church. The magnificent buildings were designed by many of the great Italian Renaissance masters including Michelangelo, Bramante and Gianlorenzo Bernini.

A dented *Volkswagen bus* crept its way through the square and stopped near the bottom of the giant

Basilica. The side door of the vehicle slid open to reveal a young boy, who stepped out eagerly, took a few seconds to position himself at the bottom of one of the large Bernini columns, and then proceeded to urinate freely on its base.

The most reverend Archbishop Manuel Zagranski, emerging from the church, was disgusted seeing the boy exposed. "Move along there!" he ordered. "Have you no respect for God and His holy property? Get along now!" Muttering curses, he motioned the child away.

The driver of the van swore bitterly at the greying Polish priest in the black cassock and the child was pulled back inside by an older girl. The van chugged away into the middle of the old square and stopped near a street vendor opening his stand for the day.

The middle-aged, highly irritated archbishop strode through the busy courtyard to the elaborate metal gates leading onto the Via della Conciliazione. He paused briefly to look back and saw that the van was still there in violation of his holy orders, and that the child was finishing his business right next to the fountains. Zagranski was furious. Peeing in Saint Peter's Square showed a complete lack of respect not only for him but for the mother church. He turned away disgusted.

The apartment he was going to was near the San Pietro Cafe and enroute he passed many more ignorant peasants whose vile actions defied his unspoken holy instructions. Their time would come, he promised himself. He would make all the filthy vagrants of the world pay for their transgressions. They were all evil and were desecrating the holy city he loved so much.

In five minutes, he reached his destination and walked up two flights of stairs to the church-owned apartment. Three plainclothes guards greeted him stiffly. "Has everyone arrived?" he asked coldly.

"Yes, your Eminence," answered the tallest.

"Good. Make damn sure we're not interrupted."

"Yes, your Eminence."

Two reinforced doors opened and he passed by an Opus Dei guard carrying an Italian-issue automatic rifle. Briskly, he continued to the innermost chamber, a spacious conference room with cameras monitoring every seat around the table. The only vacant one was at the head of the table. He was greeted by the slightly irritating cacophony of several different languages being spoken, but the room turned silent as soon as he sat down. The doors were closed and locked behind him by one of the guards while another closed the dark red drapes and turned on the ceiling lights.

"Good morning, everyone," the archbishop said gravely in English, looking at each one of the twelve men individually. He was seated next to his confidante, Bishop Juan Carlos Ruiz. "It seems we have serious issues to address. Besides Cardinal Hernandez, a substantial amount of money has been stolen from us. We will discuss what to do about these situations in a few minutes. First and foremost though, it appears that Leigh Rovarik and his people have our relic. He is a heretic, this Gypsy priest. He is vile and those helping him are blasphemers. We must not let him have his way with us. We must recover the cloth and begin our mission to rid the world of these evils. Please open your briefs so that we can consider our alternatives. Remember, as you read, that our only goal is to protect and serve the church as we have been directed to do by Father Escriva and the *Work of God* movement."

TWENTY

Paris
October 22

Robert and Sophie have 'the Key'
But they still need to solve Two Parts of a puzzle —
A Number Sequence Code a Password

The world of the 1990s seemed to be moving on fast forward and the turmoil taking place everywhere was insane. It was possible to escape it briefly in places like the Sisters of the Holy Angels convent in Canada or Abby's house on the Vineyard, but removing oneself entirely from the madness was almost impossible.

The rapid changes of the information infrastructure in the '80s and '90s had affected everyone. Technology and communications companies had amassed incredible power and their directors were making changes so fast that people were being robbed of many of their freedoms without realizing it. For some, materialism had become a god, and the almighty a circuit board. It seemed as if those who were out of control had taken control of everything.

Sophie found herself brutally re-entering this world as the American Airlines 767 jet taxied on the airstrip at Orly airport in France. Robert, seated beside her, squeezed her hand in apparent consolation as the wheels of the aircraft slowed it to a stop. They both knew it was the end of Sophie's sojourn.

Waiting to disembark, Sophie thought about how she would rather be enjoying the wonderful sights of Paris under different circumstances or be back at the convent nourishing her soul. But neither choice was an option. She had few now. The Slavic priest and Robert had convinced her that she had to come back here and face her tormentors or they would come to her. The only consolation was that Robert was with her and Jamie was waiting outside to drive them into the city. It was nice to have good friends.

Depending on traffic, it can take between 45 minutes and two hours to drive to the city from the airport. Paris is well known for traffic congestion and accidents are a common occurrence. Driving in, Jamie was prepared for delays, but to his surprise traffic moved along smoothly. His theory, as he told it to Sophie and Robert, was that most people were probably in church.

Forty minutes after leaving Orly he guided the Audi past the *Rue Haxo* and into the heart of Paris. At the *Champs Elysees*, things changed. Cars appeared from everywhere, their drivers honking loudly, swearing violently, and lurching in all directions trying to get ahead of one another. It appeared that church had let out.

After crossing the Seine River, they turned onto the Rue Gregoire de Tours near the Saint Germain des Pres Square. Jamie was exhausted and relieved to finally get to the Latin Quarter. He was almost claustro*phobic* about driving and hated Paris traffic the most. He parked in front of a small shop and, after peering up and down the street, opened the back door for Sophie and Robert to get out.

He was well aware of the watery symptoms of stress taking place externally upon him but ignored them. His focus was more inward, thankful that he didn't have to continue to navigate through the masses of cars speeding like disturbed insects in a pattern only they knew. Driving was the one thing in life he would absolutely rather not do.

Number 8 Rue Gregoire de Tours was the Artisans des Monasteres de Bethlehem building, an old brick structure with splintered pine trim marked by years of sun and storm, and three curved windows in the front. Out of habit, Sophie stopped to browse the windows. On the right were eight elegant porcelain dishes. In the center were two statues: a tiny Madonna and a large St. Guillaume. The left window held small icons of cloth, porcelain and metal, mostly silver, as well as a few crosses. Everything looked delicate.

Robert and Jamie entered the shop with Sophie trailing right behind them. The inside was dusty and some of the display cases were covered up with cloths. Clearly, this place was not regularly open for business. The statues of the saints and the Christ child were all that greeted them.

"I thought you said someone was meeting us here," Jamie remarked, "Because Sophie and you have '*the key*' with you to get into the *secret account* at the *Knights Private Bank* — all you two have to do is figure out a *Number Sequence Code and the Password*."

"Someone is supposed to," said Robert. They both seemed to find the scene eerie.

"What time did you tell him we would arrive?" Sophie asked.

Robert looked at his watch. It was ten-thirty. "About eleven o'clock. We're early."

Jamie breathed a sigh of relief and remembered that it should have taken them longer to get here. But Sophie felt tense, expecting something to go wrong. Being back in Europe, so close to those who were chasing her, was not comfortable.

Robert tried to calm her. "He'll be here. We are early," he said reassuringly.

As his words reverberated in the silence, others broke the stillness. "Bonjour, mes amies. We have been waiting upstairs for you. I'm glad you made it here without incident. I hope you did not mind this roundabout route. It is the safest road back in. I'm sure Zagranski's people are watching all flights from the States into London." The three turned to see Father Leigh Rovarik and, moving slowly behind him, Father Timothy Childs.

"It is good to see you all here safe. Please settle yourselves now, children," Father Leigh said. "You are in good hands again and everything is in order." Timothy appeared too ill to do anything but nod his head weakly, extend his hand slightly and sit down.

Father Rovarik blessed himself as he passed by a statue of Christ and took a small, ornate crucifix on a gold chain from its hook on the wall. Holding it out, he again made the sign of the cross. "I think this will be of help to you, Sophie." He gently secured it around her neck, brushed away her hair, and kissed her forehead. Then he held her face tenderly in his big hands, like a loving father holds his child. "I've noticed you do not wear one of these and wonder if you would be kind enough to indulge an old man who knows beyond a doubt that our faith in Christ's goodness and forgiveness is all that separates us from evil and those who wish to do us harm. Without belief in His guidance, we will certainly all fail in our holy mission."

Sophie didn't know what to say or do but held herself still so that he could finish. Then he extended his right arm to the rest of the group. With two fingers extended in a gesture of blessing, he made the sign of the cross and softly directed them to the rear exit. "I think it's time I told you about the Knights and the significance of a cruciform, square crosses and objects linked to the *Blood of Jesus Christ* like *The Turin Shroud* and *The Holy Grail*. We had better get along now, children. ***It is time to return to London***."

TWENTY-ONE

En route to London from Paris
October 24

The relic contains 'the Blood of Jesus Christ'

Leigh Rovarik fastened his seat belt and readied himself for the hour-long *flight to London*. He placed an overnight bag under the seat in front of him and made sure his valise was resting securely beside him. Instinctively, he moved his right foot forward to rest it on the bag. It made him feel better to have it there.

The past two days had been especially wearing on him and his body was beginning to show signs of stress. He folded his hands for a moment of reflection, praying for continued strength, knowing that things were going to get more tense, not less, from now on. There had been worse times though, he told himself, and he had made it through all of them. Everything would work out now, too. He trusted in Jesus to guide him. To give in to doubt would be foolish, a breach of his faith in God and His wisdom and goodness, and he never questioned God's holy will—only *man's selfishness and stupidity*.

He prayed silently, bowing his head while keeping one eye on the bag at his feet. He asked Christ for the courage to finish what had to be done for the mother church. Then he sat back and looked out at the clouds, pondering the ways of the Lord, thinking it wasn't just coincidence that had brought Sophie and Timothy together in Vermont. He remembered how misguided Timothy had become by the hollowness of the 1970s. Thinking it was the right time to change the world, he had foolishly taken the precious artifact from Galilee.

Although it seemed like an eternity now, it was only yesterday that Timothy had led him to his hiding place: a moldy trunk in the wine cellar of a Chantonnay Franciscan church 50 kilometers from Paris. After they had recovered the cloth, Leigh took Timothy to a private Catholic hospital. The decrepit priest's body and senses were giving out and he needed rest badly. At first he had resisted but upon reflection, he had realized that he could best help everyone by getting himself out of the way. He trusted Father Rovarik to do what was necessary.

Leigh opened his valise and carefully lifted out some worn pages from a notebook. Again, he read the descriptions of a different cloth:

"The *Turin Shroud* is three-feet-seven-inches wide and fourteen-feet-three inches long. Records of it date back to the ninth century, when it was recorded as being in Jerusalem. In the twelfth century, it was described as being in Constantinople. After a brief stay in Belgium, it became the property of the House of Savoy in 1474. In 1532, the shroud was damaged by fire. Three years later, it was moved to Turin. This was followed by brief movements around Europe until its return to Turin in 1706. In

1946, without relinquishing ownership, Hubert II of Savoy entrusted the shroud to the Archbishop of Turin. The first photographs of the shroud were taken in 1898. Official photographs were taken in 1931."

Leigh continued reading and compared the description of the Turin Shroud with the cloth he recovered yesterday. Their sizes and materials were somewhat the same. He leafed through more papers and stopped at the reproduction of a letter written by Professor Max Frie, a well known criminologist and scientist from Zurich, Switzerland. Frie had been commissioned by the Catholic Church to authenticate and date the Turin Shroud. In 1969, in a letter to the Vatican, he had summarized his initial evaluations.

"I have found some tiny grains of fossilized pollens from vegetation which existed in and around Palestine some twenty centuries ago. In addition, remnants of other plants which grew in the areas of Constantinople and the Mediterranean have been identified. To date, pollens from fifteen plant varieties have been found. Six are from Palestine, one from Constantinople, and eight from the Mediterranean area. Although it is too early to be conclusive, we strongly suspect that the *origins of the Turin Shroud can be traced to the time of Christ*, which makes it possible that it is authentic."

He picked up a 1976 description of the shroud from an Italian newspaper, correlating Frie's early findings with more recent ones from a team of scientists who used more sophisticated equipment.

"After a seven-year investigation of the Turin Shroud, said to have covered Christ's body, a group of scientists have concluded that based on its age it is not authentic: it is a forgery. In addition, '*the bloodstains*' found on the Turin cloth *are from a person who was still alive at the time the stains were made.*"

Rovarik returned the pages to the worn valise and thought about the discoveries that had not been included in any news releases. For instance, Max Frie had been correct in saying that minute traces of certain healing agents, including ancient varieties of sage and verbena, had been found in the shroud. These plants were known to have been used for healing wounds by physicians in Palestine at the time of Christ. It was common knowledge in the church now that, in their effort to replicate the real shroud, whoever had fabricated the Turin copy had discovered some interesting facts about the original one.

"*The trick to any good forgery is to try to duplicate the original work as closely as possible, is it not*? If we accept the fact that *the original work was used as a model,* then we must ask ourselves: Why does one try to heal the wounds of a corpse?" Speaking softly to himself, Rovarik recited the exact questions posed by one of the scientists in an interview he had attended.

Like most people, Leigh knew now that the Turin Shroud was a remarkable imitation of the one thought to have existed. He knew also that someone had painstakingly reproduced what they considered to be the exact conditions of the original shroud. The medicinal herbs posed a serious problem. The whole belief system of the Catholic religion rested upon Jesus dying on the cross that terrible Friday and then being resurrected and mystically ascending into Heaven. Although scholars had rejected the Turin's authenticity, their findings presented *conflicting arguments about* the actual circumstances which surrounded the death and— *the life of Jesus Christ.*

To publish evidence strongly questioning the validity of church teachings was not considered to be in the best interests of the church and the reports had been suppressed by the Vatican. The lords of Rome did not want to hear blasphemous conjecture about *Jesus being alive* when He was taken to His burial chamber. Dismissing the findings as speculative and inaccurate, they had buried everything associated with them deep in the Vatican archives along with volumes of other information that contradicted their teachings.

It had been a dry, dusty day in 1964 when Leigh's friend, Giovanni Battista Montini—Pope Paul VI—had brought the treasure to his church in Galilee. Leigh had never seen Montini as worried as when he took him aside and informed him of what he had just done. Montini told him that he and his deacon must guard the treasure with their lives and souls. "One day," he said, *"when the merchants of the earth have taken over the temple again,"* the church would need their help desperately.

Leigh watched a series of thick white clouds pass over the wings of the aircraft. The ominous day Pope Paul VI had spoken of was here. He thought deeply about the Turin Shroud and how the cardinals had tried to discredit the information it revealed, how *they always got rid of everything and everyone who threatened them.* He glanced down at the small leather bag, thinking about the death mask of Christ and how different the cloth his sister had brought to Rome was. Then he thought about the copy Pope Paul had left for Escriva and his people, and *how easy it was to duplicate something if you have the original to use as a model.* He wondered what they were going to do to him when they found out *he had the real one.*

TWENTY-TWO

London
October 25

Everyone goes from Paris to London
They all arrive on FLEET STREET
Sophie is fearful of gargoyles-dragons

Fearsome dragons guard the entrances to old London, hellish demons perched on tall pedestals said to stop evils from entering the city. The most prominent one is on *Fleet Street* about a mile from the downtown banking and investment centers.

The *Old City*, as it is called, was rebuilt after a fire destroyed it in 1666. It is quite distinct from the other boroughs even *Westminster*, where the Royal Palaces, government buildings and the prestigious museums are located.

Sophie was still trying to get her bearings after an unsettling EuroStar train ride under the English Channel. After seeing her to a taxi Robert and Jamie had gone off in a different direction to get some necessary business done. Father Rovarik was coming in on a hired plane. As the fast-moving car headed towards Piccadilly Circus, she looked up to see *the dragon* on its *Fleet Street* perch. Her mind was spinning and she felt lost. Seeing it reminded her of the nightmares, the ones in which a gorgon haunted and hunted her on a bridge.

But in London real demons were chasing her, not creations from her unconscious mind. The devils here wore black cassocks and white collars and she knew they wouldn't go away. She held tightly onto the cross Father Rovarik had given her. He had said it would give her the courage and strength she needed and she smiled at the thought as she watched the dragon disappear behind her.

A few minutes later, seeing a familiar red double-decker bus headed towards Westminster Square, Sophie realized joyfully that some of her fear and anguish had quieted and she felt more at ease. In some ways, it was good to be home.

The suite in the Park Lane Hotel on Piccadilly Street, where she and Cardinal Hernandez had met with the Venetian, was not the address she had given the taxi driver, who was coughing incessantly during the ride. They drove past the hotel and reversed direction across from Green Park, turned onto Stratton Street and stopped at #7. Sophie paid the fare, gave the driver a one-pound tip, and then walked up to the unguarded entrance, still surprised to be feeling so calm and at ease.

The taxi cab left, but did not drive away to another fare. It stopped just up the street and the driver turned off the engine, got out and crouched down as if he was inspecting the pressure of the back tire. Something wasn't functioning properly. But it was not the car. It was his body. As hard as he tried to focus on the woman walking into the building behind him, he could not hold back the green vomit and blood. It spewed out from his mouth, sliding down against the side fender of the car and onto the cobblestones. He heaved the hated sickness repeatedly onto the street.

Wiping his face, he wondered why he hadn't just taken Sophie out. He could have done it easily and maybe even learned where the money was. But the money and Sophie were no longer his most pressing concerns. He didn't care much about the church's vendetta against this woman and her friends, or the sacred treasure. The only thing Silas Willoughby thought about was Leigh Rovarik, the priest who had somehow afflicted him with the malady he now suffered from. He knew that Sophie would eventually lead him to Rovarik.

Silas cursed the holy man, wiping again his bloody mouth, this time with his shirt sleeve. When he found Rovarik, he would first make him reveal what he had done to him and then he would make him pay dearly for it. It was the fucking priest who was killing him. Nothing and no one else mattered anymore. The church and its black-robed bank robbers could go to hell if they thought he would get them what they wanted at the cost of his own life.

An hour later, Sophie was still trying to convince herself that she was feeling comfortable now that she was back in London. She enveloped herself in the pillows of her living room couch looking through a box of notes and papers until she found the news clips she was looking for. She wanted to refresh her memory about a second group associated with the Catholic Church, not the Opus Dei but those who called themselves the Knights of Malta.

The Order of the Knights of Malta is a religious sect within the Catholic Church, tracing its origins to 11th-century Jerusalem just prior to the First Crusade. As such it is the oldest known order of chivalry in existence. The secret community was founded by Blessed Gerard and a group of warrior monks in a Jerusalem infirmary. Their mission was to tend to the sick and to promote and protect the rights of the poor.

The holy organization has espoused a variety of charitable, military and spiritual purposes since then. There have been holy and honorable times for it as well as periods when its members and goals have been less than noble. The deeds of its members are performed in the name of God and depend upon the social and spiritual conditions of the world during any time period. Members are called Soldiers of Christ. Their female counterparts are known as the Dames of Honor and Devotion.

At present, the Order of the Knights of Malta is heavily invested in maintaining political, social and economic privilege. Membership is limited to particular family lines, although exceptions are occasionally made for men and women who have achieved a high level of financial or political power. They comprise a who's who of Catholic family lines and political and financial power. Members have access to the Catholic Church hierarchy and elite international financial groups. The member lists of the Holy Order of the Knights of Malta are held privately.

Putting the article down, Sophie's anxiety returned. She had never looked upon her family's involvement in the order as being either good or bad, although she had resisted her father's pressures to socialize and do business with the Knights and their families. She had also been obstinate in her refusal to become involved in any relationships with its members. It was, in fact, a firm rule she had made for herself.

There had been one exception. It had been at her father's birthday party 10 years ago at *the family estate* just outside *Monaco*. She had been studying for her doctoral degree and was home for a term break. At the party she had been aloof, and Abby had admonished her for it and asked her to behave more graciously. One day, her aunt had said, like it or not, she might need one of these people. After a few glasses of vintage champagne, Sophie had decided to listen to her favorite aunt's advice. She would make the best of it and have a good time. She would play with them all. But things hadn't quite worked out that way because it was at this rather dull party, while she was being her most menacing self, that she met the alluring man from Cyprus.

When she first saw Andre Macheras, she had been flirting with a dull Frenchman. Andre was standing by the gardens talking *business with her father* and another gentleman. Sophie recalled the scene exactly. How incredibly handsome Andre was, his complexion darkened by the sun and his eyes, even from a distance, sparkling like the stars in the sky above her. He was tall, thin, and greying, and looked not only supremely confident but wonderfully dignified. He was the most attractive man Sophie had seen in a long time. Once she had set her mind to it, it had taken her only 15 minutes to monopolize his attention. Without wasting time on an introduction she had walked over, interrupted the conversation and invited him to dance.

The rest was history. They had courted over the next several days, then flown to *Ibiza* on holiday. It was a deliriously happy month for Sophie. Andre had made her feel different, more valued, than anyone had before. He had catered to her every need and talked with her about her real feelings and innermost thoughts. And he never lied to her about anything, not even about his wife and children and their love for each other. After weeks of bliss he told her that he would be returning to Cyprus. They had spent the last few days and nights vowing to continue their relationship at a distance, but they hadn't.

Sophie picked up the news clip that described Andre Macheras as an enigmatic figure from Cyprus, a prominent member of the Knights of Malta and one of the richest people in Europe.

The next time she had spoken to Andre had been years later, after she'd joined the Opus Dei, when she had decided to take their money. Knowing that she had to hide it somewhere, she had thought of him. Perhaps it had been her state of mind or her desperate need for someone to care about her. Robert seemed to have changed and their relationship had gone sour, even before her affair with the cardinal. Having few choices, she had called Andre advised her to get the money into bank accounts out of the country. He had also warned her against taking the money. The Opus Dei, he said, would find a way to get it back and would kill her to keep their secrets quiet. She was adamant, however. Finally, he told her that accounts could be set up in her name in his Cyprus banks. The money would be safe—and for her own well-being she should come to Cyprus.

She had agreed only to part of it. She set up transfer routes redirecting the money from the Opus Dei foundations in London into new accounts at Andre's banks, but she never went to Cyprus. She did not want to expose him or his family to the danger she knew she was in.

In moving the money to Andre, into his *Knights private bank*, she had trusted him with her life. She smiled to herself, thinking that in some way she had actually listened to her Aunt Abby's advice at the party. And now, reaching for the wireless telephone, it was time to see whether the trust she had placed in Andre Macheras, the man whom she would always love, had been a good idea.

TWENTY-THREE

London
October 26

The Code is deciphered by Robert and Sophie
The Number Sequence Code 'is Simple'
The Password has Five Letters and is linked
— to Sophie

While Sophie had been contemplating the reports from Andre Macheras and Father Leigh Rovarik was enroute to London with the relic, Robert was at his Pembridge Court flat in London drinking too much coffee, planning what he thought would be a complicated electronic money recovery process. Between sips, he was trying to figure out what Andre had done with Sophie's money.

Sophie had called him the previous night to tell him that Andre had finally returned her call to him. During the course of their conversation, Andre had said he'd had to make significant changes in their business arrangements and had withdrawn her money from his banks and deposited it elsewhere. He had been quite circumspect about it. She would receive a package shortly, he told her, which would explain the details of what he had done; she shouldn't worry. He asked her to call him back after she'd had a chance to look at the contents of the parcel. Then he had ended the call by saying that she should come to Cyprus as soon as possible to discuss some remaining issues.

Robert's anxiety swelled. He neither liked nor trusted this charismatic banker from Cyprus. "Bankers don't make changes without cause and they especially don't move funds around without trying to consult with the account owner," he fumed. A wave of jealousy came over him.

As he was entering the last of the account numbers from the microfilm into his computer, the doorbell rang. His chair squeaked as he rose to answer it. He walked to the door, worrying that Sophie's microfilmed information might prove to be useless. The courier she had sent handed him the package. After seeing him out, Robert put it on his desk top and removed a handful of well-organized papers from it. He looked first at the alphabetized lists of about 50 banks, then at the identifying tags for the account numbers at each. He assumed that the Cypriot had assigned the new numbers.

Attached to the sheets was a short laser-printed note to Sophie: "Please find enclosed the institutions involved and the bank account numbers which will confirm our new arrangements. I remember well the time and the love we shared together in Milan. I will love you always."

Judging from the hastiness of the transfers and the fact that none of the new banks were in Cyprus; Robert assumed that something had gone wrong. Something other than the intermittent wars that took place between Greece and Turkey. He noted that all of the new banks were small, provincial European institutions. This made sense. None of these banks had access to high-speed information systems, nor were they directly linked to larger banks' computers. The high-speed electronic equipment of the larger banks made it difficult to conceal interbank transfers and most of them were not only linked together but inspected frequently by regulators looking for illegal transactions. Large transfers of funds, money crossing international borders, and multiple currency exchanges are wonderful opportunities for illegal activity, and they would have spotted these.

Robert decided to begin his own investigation by figuring out whether the money was where Macheras claimed it to be. He began by assuming that the banks listed were genuine and that the numbers would match up with the microfilmed account numbers created last year. Logically, the access routes into the new accounts would use some combination of old and new numbers. He knew that he would have to match the old numbers with the new ones and then figure out the password.

Not long after he started, he looked away from the monitor confused. Things weren't making sense. It should have been difficult to get into the new accounts.

Or they could have been chimeras with no money in them at all. But it appeared that neither was the case. The account number combinations went together too easily; the first two and last two digits of each set were exactly the same.

The password, too, *was* ludicrously *simple*. A child could have seen it. It had to do with Sophie's affair with Andre. Once he had thoroughly convinced her that he was no longer interested in the Opus Dei and could be trusted, Sophie had told him every detail about their relationship, how they'd met, their monthlong love affair, and everything she could recall about their recent financial dealings, including her steps in redirecting the Opus Dei money to his banks. He had stifled his jealousy and they had tried not to overlook anything in their discussions. Robert thought the password might be a date, room number, or something else they both knew about that no one else did. When he saw the note Andre sent to her he knew what it was. "I cherish the time and love we shared together in Milan. I will love you always," it read. Sophie and Andre had not been in Italy together; they had gone to *Ibiza*, an island off the coast of Spain.

Within two hours, Robert had attached himself by modem to most of the new banks. A few hours later, he had accessed up-to-date account balance information from each and merged the data into one file. He sorted and printed it out as a consolidated report with transaction summaries and present accounts balances. Most of the money, he saw, had been transferred from Andre's banks in bits and pieces, presumably to conceal the large sums involved. The new accounts were all non-interest bearing so there would be no income reports. Each deposit had been charged a 15 percent handling fee, a normal commission for cleaning money. That came as no surprise.

Reaching the end of the totals sections, he was amazed to see that the available funds appeared to be accessible. The access routes seemed to be wide open, although he couldn't be certain until he tried to withdraw the monies, which could take him several days. All sorts of things could go wrong when he tried to do this, but it looked like nothing would. Hours later, he was still trying to figure out why everything was being made so easy.

The simplicity of it reminded him of the bank frauds in the 1980s that had helped create the U.S. savings and loan debacle. Reputable business people had run that scam. Their game was simple: They deposited their own money into small rural banks, took out unsecured loans using their checking accounts as their only collateral, withdrew their funds from the banks, and defaulted on the loans. Then they watched the bank's collapse, and bought their own bad debts back, at a discount, from the purchasers of the banks' assets. Bankers and businessmen shared information about such things as this, he thought. The phrase "Brothers in Malta" came to mind when he thought of such things.

Still, it took a long time for him to get even reasonably comfortable with what he saw on his computer screen. It wasn't just that he was nervous about the impending transactions he was going to try to make.

It was that it should have taken a lot longer to get at the information. There should have been some roadblocks put in place. Although money laundering was supposed to be simple like this—almost boring—it usually wasn't.

In theory, you find the right person to put the dirty money into the wash for you and it comes out clean, dry and folded. But in the world of bad business, nothing ever goes the way it should. People get greedy. They go crazy. They even kill each other. The more money involved and fingers in the till, the more likely it is that something will go wrong. "Confusion is opportunity," a friend had once said. "It's how we all make money." But here, no confusion was being created, and what was worse, no one was getting greedy. It was bothersome.

Robert didn't usually smoke but Jamie had left an open pack of cigarettes on the table next to him and he took one out, lit it up and blew tiny rings of smoke into the air around him. "Christ, he's just about *piecing the* fucking *numbers together* for us and *giving us the code word*. People don't do things this way unless there's a good reason to." He thought that Andre Macheras was reeling him in one move at a time. Why? What was he after? Or was he afraid?

In trying to decide whether the Cypriot was after something or was scared, Robert remembered the strong messages sent out by the Sicilian mafia about anyone stealing money from them or their friends at the IOR and the Vatican. He had heard the London bobbies took Leonardo Roberto Calvi down from his neck hanging not far from where he was right now for doing just that. Maybe that was the reason for Andre's generosity: He wanted to stay alive.

After 15 minutes of mulling this over, Robert's thoughts shifted away from Andre Macheras and the actions of the Vatican's executioners to something different. He thought that Sophie was relying on him to help her get herself out of this, yet her tone of voice and something she'd said this morning indicated that she had some doubts about him. He knew, because of what she said that she was regaining her confidence and becoming stronger each day. In fact, she'd sounded much more like her old self when, after telling him she loved him, she'd said, "There isn't much time left—I'll give you one full day to figure this out, Robert, and if you don't have it worked out by then, I'll take over. I can use that computer as well as you can."

She won't have the opportunity, he said to himself, refocusing his concentration on the computer screen. No problem, he thought, but the first thing I need to do is be a bit creative, and this will involve the fabrication of a little entity which is called *a private bank*.

TWENTY-FOUR

October 28

The secret at the Knight's Private Bank

Private banking is not a new concept in the world of money management.

The fabulously wealthy have always had personal banking advisors to counsel them. Money makes money, but only if it is handled properly by the right people. The old rich of the world have traditionally used the proprietors of only a select group of commercial banks, investment houses and holding companies to do this. To be on one of their client lists absolutely guarantees that one's money will be well tended to. In controlling these outcomes, the investment firms employ thousands of market analysts who process complex financial data generated daily from specific trade areas. The bankers evaluate the information provided to them and move their patrons' investments around accordingly. Information is power and the power of the banking wizards, with their well-established lock on the funds of the fabulously wealthy families, is quite considerable.

Since the years of the Bush presidency, however, a new group of investment brokers has emerged, their ascent directly related to the increased numbers of the new rich, those people who have made their fortunes within the past 30 or 40 years. Although wealthy, their total worth and financial values are relatively small compared to the old rich. Despite capital holdings that are quite significant by anyone's standards, most of them do not begin to qualify for entry into the high-stake investment clubs of the rule-setters, the old banking firms. To put it bluntly, they're not allowed in. The new investors, therefore, are aggressively courted by an odd assortment of law firms, commercial banks, and brokerage houses offering a wide array of capital management services and unique investment plans. The most successful of these to date are the private banks.

The bank that Robert created on his computer had nothing to do with investing the money of the new rich, however. It was designed with only one purpose in mind: to process and accept Sophie's money back without anyone knowing it. Once this had been accomplished, he would be able to move the money quickly into something more permanent, close the doors of *the bank* forever and throw away *the keys*.

It did not take long to set everything up. After calling Sophie to keep her informed about what he was doing, he phoned some friends with connections to the right people. These shady characters were part of a banking coalition that had evolved after the famous Bank of Credit and Commerce International scandal. They had been middle-level players in that devious game with no direct ties to the major players. But like a lot of others, they had reeled in significant profits from the bank's fallout. And they always had things for sale. Robert presumed that their present laundry list probably included a few inactive bank charters.

He was right. They had quite a number for sale. The one he chose was an older bank called The Banque Original. It was included on a banks-for-sale list provided to him by one of these friends. After looking at the list he didn't have to think twice about his selection. This bank suited his needs perfectly.

Most of its business had been done in northern Cyprus and it had officially ceased operations about 20 years ago. Like Andre Machera's thinking, his own was well calculated. And, Andre's participation in this game played a large role in his decision: If anyone did any checking, they would assume that the Cypriot was somehow involved and by the time they figured out that he wasn't, Robert would be long gone.

Twelve hours later, Robert had bought and reactivated the old bank charter. It was officially registered by his friends at the Banking Commission in London as operating again. The new Statement of Principals certificate showed a subsidiary branch at 50 Curzon Street, London, England. The suite on Curzon Street was an expensive office that Robert leased from a discreet English businessman. It came equipped with phones, up-to-date computer systems and all the office equipment he needed. His suite was made to look and function exactly like any other private banking operation. And for a little extra money, a routing system that was capable of receiving and sending wire transfers was set up and linked to a private corporation's satellite.

Although the European banks which held Sophie's money had obsolete equipment, Robert hoped he would be able to recover the money using the special linkages he had installed. To be successful in banking, one simply had to be innovative. In this case that meant having access to the right information and choosing the right telecommunications company to process the withdrawals.

After he was comfortable that everything was functioning properly, Robert left the office to get some fresh air. He walked out onto Curzon Street whistling a verse from a song by Arlo Guthrie, "You can get anything you want at *Alice's Restaurant*." The world is absolutely an Alice's Restaurant, he thought, if you have enough money and know the right people.

TWENTY-FIVE

October 30

***Silas is captured by Robert, Sophie and Leigh
'A miracle happens to Silas'***

Leigh Rovarik shuffled wearily up the steep steps to Sophie's third-floor apartment, worrying about her situation and her relationship with Robert Hathaway. Breathing heavily from the climb, he knocked softly on her door.

Sophie was surprised and overjoyed to see him standing there. "I didn't want to alarm you, my child, but there are some things we must talk about, in private." He tried to calm her with his fatherly reassurances and arm-in-arm they walked into her living room.

"I was wondering when you'd get to London, Father. I've seen the Gypsies milling around outside for days now." She took his black overcoat and hat and invited him to relax in a comfortable-looking armchair. "Let me get you something hot to drink, Father, please."

When she returned with tea, he said, "It is advisable that we be careful." His eyes never left hers.

He motioned for her to sit opposite him and noticed that she was wearing the cross he had given her. He wasted no time getting directly to the point. "You have told me that besides the money and securities you received here from the man from Venice, some tape recordings and copies of church records were involved. Would you be kind enough, my child, to describe these things in detail to me?"

Only a few streets away, Robert wasn't humming the lyrics to any tunes when he left the office this time. Like the old priest, he was struggling to stay calm. He was also absentminded and had just neglected, as he left the bank for the final time, to put out the lights and lock the doors. But his carelessness was understandable. He was in a hurry for good reason.

Sophie's flat on Stratton was a block away from the Curzon Street office and usually only a five-minute walk. But tonight wasn't even close to being a normal night. It was important for Robert to get to Sophie as quickly as possible to tell her what he'd done. Breaking into a sprint, he rounded the corner of Stratton Street and looked up to the third-floor apartment. The front room light was yellow a signal that meant Sophie was there, waiting for him.

Robert didn't notice the gaping pothole in the road in front of him. It was dark and foggy, and he wasn't watching where he was going. His *right foot* slipped on the cobblestones and *his ankle twisted out* from under him. He spun around, first sideways, then backwards, and before he could regain his balance, he hit the road hard. For a moment he thought he'd been shot. He lay motionless, afraid to move. After a few seconds, he nervously searched himself for blood but found nothing.

Pain signals from the peripheral nerves in his *right ankle* provided the first indication to him that *he was injured.* He dragged himself up onto the sidewalk, feeling nauseous. He heard something, a voice shouting at him from across the street. A stranger had witnessed his crash and was repeating his concern for Robert's well-being.

"Are you all right? Can you talk?" Robert looked up to see someone coming towards him through the dense fog. "Are you hurt bad, man?"

"I'm not sure," Robert answered matter-of-factly, still wondering himself.

"Should I call someone? You look like you've injured yourself."

"No. That isn't necessary. Thank you. I'm fine, really. Just a little shaken up, that's all."

Robert wasn't at all sure that he was fine, and he allowed himself to be helped up by the stranger. As he tried to focus on the man's face, he realized that his vision was blurry. He tried to put some weight on his injured ankle, and the contorted expression on his face reflected the severity of the discomfort. His voice followed suit and he screamed out loudly in response to the pain shooting through his body. "God damn it!"

"Jesus. Can I help you to get somewhere, man? Is there any place I can take you? A hospital? Christ, you're hurt, man." The stranger persisted in his offers of kindly assistance.

Robert looked up at Sophie's windows. He had to get there without more delay. It would be easier and quicker with the stranger's assistance. He pointed to the third floor. "Yes, I was on my way to that flat. I have friends there who'll take care of me."

One man's calamity can be another's fortune. As it turned out, the stranger wasn't just a good Samaritan. For him, the accident was a stroke of luck.

The banging on the door caught Sophie and Father Rovarik completely off guard. They had been deeply involved in discussion and it was hard to say whose face registered the most surprise when they cautiously opened the door. Sophie saw only Robert, who was leaning against a man behind him, and took his outstretched hand to help him inside. Father Rovarik hardly even noticed Robert. His sight was firmly fixed on the man in the rear, the one who had been stalking him for weeks now.

Silas shoved *Robert* forcefully into the hall. Then, with a movement of his right arm, he flicked *Sophie* out of his way, and made straight for the man from Galilee. He gripped him by the throat with one hand and *put a gun* to his face with the other. He cocked the hammer and at the same time ordered Sophie to close and latch the door behind him. After she complied, he ordered her to lie on the floor next to where Robert had fallen, warning that if either did anything stupid, all three would pay a price. Then he directed his attention back to the priest.

"Remember me, you holy prick?" The vulgar words were whispered softly into the priest's ears, along with the disgusting smell of sputum. "I have been waiting a long time for this moment. You and I have something to settle Rovarik." Silas spun the priest around and marched him in the direction of the living room. He motioned for Sophie to follow and to bring Robert with her.

"What do you want from us?" Sophie demanded, hoping he was just a street thug.

It was *Father Rovarik's* rasping voice that answered her. "He wants nothing from you, my child. He is after something he thinks I can give him. Something he needs to survive. Just do as he says. Have faith in God and everything will be all right."

Five minutes later, *Robert and Sophie were on the living room floor, propped up against the couch* and bound with cord. Rovarik, however, was not tied up. He was seated in the same chair he had vacated minutes earlier, although not quite as comfortably now. He was trying to explain *to Silas* why he should reform his ways and become part of their pilgrimage.

"I saw, when you came to my church in Galilee, that you had been marked. The symptoms of the malady appear almost immediately. The signs are visible to anyone who has seen them before." His voice was filled with compassion.

"What do you mean, 'marked?'" Silas barked.

"It's an old Gypsy expression, Silas. It means you've been cursed."

"Cursed. For Christ's sakes, priest, that's fucking witchcraft. You don't think I believe you had someone put a spell on me, do you? What do you take me for, an idiot, Rovarik?"

"Quite the contrary, I know you're a highly intelligent operative. The Opus Dei people chose you. They didn't trust anyone else to recover the relic, did they? They are not foolish men, my son. Zagranski would not send someone after me who is not capable."

"I'm not interested in your left-handed compliments about my qualifications, priest. Cut the crap. I'm not in the mood. What do you know about what's wrong with me?" Silas was trying to be as commanding as possible under the circumstances, but he wasn't feeling well. He moved his gun to Sophie's right temple as a signal that things were going to get more tense, quickly.

The unintimidated priest went on. "You're right; however that it is not a spell or black magic. What has made you ill is your lack of belief in God and in His holy will, Silas. You have chosen for yourself a path that does not lead to God. It is the path that is cursed, not you."

"Let's be straight with each other, shall we, Rovarik? Time's wasting. I have no intention of debating with you the philosophical aspects of anything I am or do. I don't believe in your God. I think all of you priests are fucking crazy. But I've made a very good living off your conflicts. That's not why I'm here now though. The only thing that concerns me is that you have somehow gotten the upper hand with me. My guard was down somewhere and you got in. That's all. But—paths cursed, God's wishes, spells, Gypsy legends—I don't give a good goddamn about any of that crap. The truth is that if you don't give me what I need within the next 30 seconds, I'm going to rearrange this girl's lovely head. That's simple reality, Rovarik. There's no magic in seeing someone's fucking brains blown all over the room." Silas finally had the priest cornered and made an effort to enjoy every minute of it.

"Your violence is not reality, Silas. It is a mask. An illusion. The devil's hand at play disguising the truth." Rovarik paused. "Actual reality is not so simple. It encompasses many things. Parts of it we can understand, touch and feel. But some things will always be a mystery. It is God's wish that life be like this."

"You're pushing your luck, Rovarik. Tell me what I want to know or you're going to see just how real violence can be." The desperate look on Silas's face told the priest that it was time to get to the point.

"Do you remember kissing the holy rock in the Golgotha Chapel in the Church of the Holy Sepulcher?"

"Continue." Silas eased off slightly, sensing the approach of his answer.

"Many people whose souls are fouled with sin get sick when they enter the house of God, Silas. It is not unusual for them to get ill when they come so close to God or His Son." The old priest was sending his own messages out.

"Don't play games with me, Rovarik. The lady's life is on the line."

Father Rovarik saw the fury and the intense confusion. He observed also the drooping facial muscles and the lip contortions on the right side of Silas's face.

"Do you remember the disheveled looking cripple who was taking care of the flower arrangements at the holy shrine?"

"Go on, priest."

"Do you remember the old man who wiped the holy stone before and after you kissed it, Silas?" Leigh sat forward, engaging his enemy directly.

"What did you put on it, Rovarik?" He was beginning to get a glimpse of what had transpired.

"I had nothing to do with it, my son. My brother's men were protecting me. One of them infiltrated the Opus Dei group at the Hilton. He knew you would eventually come at me. Do you understand now what I mean by your path being cursed?"

"What was it? What did they do to me?" Silas grabbed at Sophie's hair and pulled her head backwards, exposing the front of her head to his weapon.

"It's an old herbal remedy for unwanted interferences, Silas. The concoction affects the central nervous system. One dose produces severe changes in the body's cellular chemistries. The long-term effects are degenerative—and deadly."

"Is there an antidote to it?" Silas slurred his words.

"There is a cure. Let's say that given the right set of circumstances, the condition you have is reversible."

"Do you have it? Is it another drug?"

"I didn't say it was a chemical, Silas. It's actually quite a different kind of remedy."

"Do you think I'm an idiot, Rovarik? I want it and I want it now, or I'll dispense with you three first and then go after your families. If I go down, you're all going with me."

Silas's hand began to quiver, a sign that another tremor was beginning. Rovarik ignored the threats.

"The way back to health is complicated, Silas. It is both a physical and a spiritual journey. You must trust that we will keep our end of the bargain and give you what you need."

"What bargain?" Silas was nauseous and dizzy again. He tried to remain focused and not pay attention to the agitation taking place throughout his body.

The priest continued to calmly pressure him, seeing clearly his weakness. "The agreement that we must all make now, Silas. It's simple really. We will give you what you are asking for and you will contact your employers in Rome and file a report that I will prepare for you. After that, you will go away to a neutral corner forever."

"No deal, priest." Silas's voice wavered. Pale red spittle found its way out of his mouth onto the lapel of his overcoat.

"Then kill us now and be done with it, my son. And find out where this path takes you." The priest held his ground, remembering the day in Germany when other persecutors had tortured him. He was supremely confident that they were all resting not so comfortably in Hell now.

Silas knew he had two choices. He could murder them all now and he himself would be dead soon, one way or another. Or he could go along with the priest, hoping he would keep his divine word and then, once he got the antidote from him, he could always settle up. But down deep, he knew his time was up. Revenge was sweet but not if the price was too high. More than anything, Silas wanted to be well again and live. "What guarantees do I have, priest?"

"My promise as a servant of God is that we will take care of you and help you to make yourself better. It is time to heal, my son, in more ways than one. But it is a choice you must make for yourself." He chastised the man with the distorted conscience one last time, knowing that the confrontation was over.

Silas lowered his shaking hand to the table, unbidden tears of defeat and relief forming in his eyes. He had tried as hard as he could to fight but the energy moving against him here was the same he had felt in the Church of the Holy Sepulcher when his life had begun to change forever. And it was as powerful and overwhelming now as it had been then. The helpless mercenary knew that something he could not explain was going on.

"At times in our lives we really don't make our own decisions do we, Silas. Destiny decides for us our alternatives," Father Leigh whispered in his ears. Then he rose and walked slowly to the hall, where he had left his coat and a small travel bag. Remembering Christ's words, "Love your enemies," he returned with the holy cloth and draped it lovingly around Silas's shoulders, saying nothing more.

A gentle warmth flowed through the room. It seemed for an instant as if time stopped altogether.

Everyone, including Silas, felt the power of the magnificent force and understood immediately that they were witnessing an event only a few in life ever do. In a small London flat, a wayward soul became the sole object of God's mighty love and was being blessed by the spirit of Jesus Christ Himself. In this case, reality was *a miracle.*

TWENTY-SIX

October 31

Silas fails in his mission and goes to a London Hospital

The head of the Opus Dei arrives from Rome on a private plane

He goes directly to the OPUS DEI HOUSE but doesn't get the secret

A clue is hidden in the 'slit of the backing' of a painting of Christ

*T*he rain was pounding down hard on the Thames River as the double-decker bus took a sharp right turn at Ranelagh Gardens* and came to a stop on *Chelsea Bridge Road.* Father Rovarik and Sophie got off and walked in the direction of the bridge. But they didn't go over it. They turned right instead onto *the*

Embankment and went west. Their destination wasn't on the other side of the river. It was on this side, two blocks away in the Embankment Gardens. *They were going to Dawliffe Hall and Shelley House, the offices of the Opus Dei* where Sophie had worked.

The most noticeable building in the area was the Buddhist Peace Pagoda, a simple, curved structure near Battersea Park and a symbol of the movement for worldwide peace and nonviolence. It stood out sharp in contrast to the rigidity of the Catholic structures on the opposite bank. As they walked, Sophie was not pondering the symbolism of the differing types of architectural styles. She was trying not to remember how awful it had been for her the last time she walked this riverbank.

Last night, when she and Father Rovarik had been talking, it had been hard for her to conjure up the old demons again, even though she had tried to, thinking it necessary. She had begun by describing her drug use, her affair with Cardinal Hernandez and the money washes through the Opus Dei foundations. But the compassionate priest had stopped her. The specifics of her indiscretions didn't interest him. He had been gentle but firm when he said, "You are not alone with your devils anymore, my child. Your sins have already been forgiven. The only thing I want you to tell me is the whereabouts of the records and *tapes* that implicate Archbishop Zagranski and Bishop Ruiz in all of this."

At first, it had taken her aback. But seeing the gleam in his eye she understood that it was time for them to cut to the chase. She had just begun to tell him the exact nature and the location of the *tapes* in Bishop Juan Carlos Ruiz's office when the knock on the door interrupted them.

Before leaving the apartment this morning, Sophie had dialed the main number at the foundation. She told the receptionist that she was a graduate student visiting London with her uncle and wanted to know more about the life of Josemarie Escriva de Balaguer. Her call had been transferred to a young priest from Madrid who said that one of the sisters who lived there would help her. And yes, a short tour of the facilities could be arranged if they arrived before noon. He had given her the names of the two nuns and said she should ask for either of them. To her relief, neither one was a familiar name. The last thing Sophie wanted was to see someone who knew her.

Sophie and Father Rovarik entered the compound through a set of bent and rusted black gates and went directly to Shelley House. Sophie was counting her paces as she climbed the granite steps up to the front doors. The girl who answered the bell, wearing a habit and a friendly smile, couldn't have been more than 19 or 20 years old.

"Father Hector Gonzalez told me to ask for Sister Rose or Sister Marie," Sophie said. "My name is Jenny Carey and this is my uncle, Edward. We're from the United States and would like to learn more about Monsignor Escriva."

"I'm Sister Rose, Miss Carey. Father Gonzalez told me you would be coming. Please come in." She opened the door wide, revealing a spacious front room with a crystal chandelier hung low in its center. Walking under it, she ushered them into the visitor's room. "Please, make yourselves comfortable," she said. "If you will be kind enough to hang your wet things in here, I will get Sister Marie. She will give you a tour of our building and can answer any questions you might have about us." She was quite formal and very pleasant.

Sophie and Father Rovarik put their sopping wet coats on a gilded coat rack in the corner. "Do you know her?" the priest whispered.

"I've never seen her before in my life. Let's hope the other one is a novice, too." Sophie nervously walked to an aquarium in the back of the room. She had once collected fish for the tank and noticed immediately that the water was cloudy. She sniffed at it and, smelling an odor, couldn't help but think that the filter should be cleaned more regularly.

"Hello, my name is Sister Marie." A middle-aged, habited woman with a very dumb smile stood in the doorway. She held several pages of what appeared to be promotional literature in one hand, and her waist rosary in the other hand.

"Father Hector told me to give these information packages to you. He prepared them for you himself." She handed them to Leigh Rovarik.

"Thank you, Sister," Sophie said, stuttering slightly. "My name is Jenny Carey and this is my uncle, Edward."

Sister Marie began her presentation as if Sophie had not spoken to her. "These brochures contain detailed explanations of the life of Josemaria Escriva de Balaguer, the founder of the Opus Dei. There is also a set which shows the actual ceremony of the beatification of the monsignor by his holiness Pope John Paul II, and a pamphlet that describes the new parish church under construction in his name in Rome." The nun looked pleased with herself.

"Thank you, Sister," Father Rovarik said. Something was awry with her introduction and he wondered whether she was medicated. Sophie, however, knew better, having gone through the Opus Dei induction process herself. She was tempted to lift up the nun's skirts to show Father Rovarik the marks the cilice makes.

"If you will both come with me." The nun talked at them, not to them, and extended her free hand towards the door. "Monsignor Escriva was born in Barbastro, Spain, on January 9, 1902. He was ordained to the priesthood in Saragossa on the 28th of March, 1925. In Madrid, on October 2, 1928, by divine inspiration he founded Opus Dei, which has opened..." opened into a large area that had been a meditation room a year ago but was now a business office. Grey screens

Father Rovarik tried to pay attention to what the nun was saying, but was more preoccupied trying to remember Sophie's description of where the bishop's office was. The hallway, lined with photographs of Josemaria Escriva, divided it into ten work stations, each equipped with a computer and a fax machine. A bank of about sixty telephones filled the two far walls, with lines and electrical wires running everywhere.

"This is the Donations Center. We use this office for our bulk mailings and one of our religious hot lines is answered here." Despite the fog she seemed to exist in, Sister Marie was able to recite her lines well.

"How many people are you contacting in a year?" Father Rovarik asked.

"Millions. Our organization is very aggressive when it comes to its mailings and telemarketing. On any given night, we have about twenty helpers making calls. They are averaging about fifty completed connections each."

"Where is the literature being sent?" Sophie asked, knowing that none of this had been going on last year.

"Everywhere, my dear. We are active in nearly every country of the world. Our literature has been translated into twelve languages. Our most recent missions have been in South America." She motioned them up the stairs.

"The remaining suites on this floor are the priests' private offices. No one is allowed to go in there. We'll go take a look at the departments, offices, residences and the chapel upstairs. This way, please."

When they got there, Sophie was gratified to see that the only thing replaced in the second-floor chapel was probably the holy water in the font at its entrance. In contrast, the first director's office they visited next had changed radically. This had been her office and all of her things were gone. But Sophie kept her face void of emotion, pretending to be only interested in the nun's tour.

"What's down there?" Father Rovarik pointed towards a walkway to their right.

"That's the corridor leading over to Dawliffe Hall. We aren't allowed over there either. If you will please follow me, I will show you our new Children's Center. It was dedicated just this past month."

About ten steps down the corridor, Sophie coughed politely and, acting embarrassed, said, "Sister Marie is there a ladies room I could use?" Letting the moment get the better of her, she added, "This morning's tea seems to have gone right through me."

"Of course, my child. It's back next to the chapel. You'll see the sign over the door. Please rejoin us at the end of this hallway, at the school, when you are through." She went on leading Rovarik as if Sophie were still there.

"The Children's Center was designed to teach our children about the importance of continuing forever the Work of God movement and the real joy of dedicating their young lives to..."

Sophie gave Rovarik a signal with a slight movement of her head, then walked back towards the ladies room. She didn't have to look for the sign. She knew exactly where it was. But she didn't go in. Hoping that no surveillance cameras had been installed in her absence, she moved directly to the corridor that was off limits.

Some things in life always seem to stay the same and some people like it that way. Bishop Juan Carlos Ruiz was one of those people. Sophie recalled the many occasions when he had lost the key to his office and had become aggressively irate. After several outbursts, he had hidden a spare key for himself. Twice, Sophie had seen him recover and use it. She had used it once herself—when she had broken into his office last year.

The Brown Code

Her conviction that the stubborn bishop wouldn't alter his ways was confirmed when she found the key tucked into a pocket near the top hinge. Her appreciation of his behavior was given a further boost as soon as she entered the room and saw *the large painting of Christ* hanging where it always had hung. *Quickly, she reached into a slit in its paper backing* and removed a thick sheaf of papers. She straightened the painting, locked the door, replaced the key and walked quickly back over to Shelley House.

The sounds of the pearl beads dragging on the floor didn't bother Sister Marie, but for Sophie they were a sign that she had escaped detection. The nun was still telling Leigh Rovarik how wonderful the foundation had been to her and how inspirational everyone associated with it was. Then she said, "Excuse me, perhaps I'd better check on your niece."

It had been awhile since Sophie had left them and just as Sister Marie was about to knock on the bathroom door, it opened and Sophie emerged.

"Is everything all right, my child?"

"Yes, Sister Marie. My stomach is a little upset, that's all. I seem to have developed a minor case of diarrhea. It must be something I ate last night." Sophie nodded to the priest that everything had gone well.

Not wanting to discuss the young lady's loose stools, Sister Marie picked up on her explanation of the organization's value system. Within five minutes, they had returned to the secretarial office and were discussing the finer points of the tour. "Is there anything else I can offer you? Any questions you might have?" she asked. She seemed to be trying to remember if she had left anything out of her lecture.

"No, Sister. I think we've seen enough. You've been most kind to help us. Thank you." The old priest looked at Sophie for a second confirmation that they had everything they came for.

"Almost," Sophie said. "I'll get our coats, Uncle Edward. Why don't you give Sister Marie a small contribution for her trouble, for the missions."

Alone in the visitors room, Sophie piled their coats and umbrella on a chair next to the door. Then she walked directly over to the fish tank. Rolling up her shirt sleeve, she put her arm down into the tank and felt along its slimy bottom for the base of a ceramic rock formation. Holding it tight, she pulled at its seal with her other hand and with some difficulty broke it off. She drew it out of the water and reached inside for the airtight plastic container that held *the tapes she had made*. She plucked it out, dried it off and dropped it into her pocketbook. Then she put the rock back in the tank so that no one would be the wiser.

Snapping up the coats and the umbrella she started back towards the secretarial office, but had taken only a few steps when she heard a loud commotion at the front door. Father Hector Gonzalez rushed into the front room and she heard him announce to Sister Rose that *the papal jet from Rome* had arrived ahead of schedule and that the two priests from the Vatican were coming in right behind him. "Have their rooms been prepared? Is everything clean and neat?" He was obviously nervous. He didn't know why the priests were here.

"Yes, Father. They are ready," Sister Rose answered, looking over his shoulder to get a glimpse of the two men emerging from the black limousine.

"Good. Where is Sister Marie?"

"Finishing up with the people from the States, Father."

As she spoke, Sister Marie walked into the front room and bowed.

"Keep her out of the way and keep her quiet," Father Hector reproached the younger nun. He went back outside and took up a formal position on the top step, hands folded, head bowed. He said nothing to the men coming up the steps.

Still in the secretary's office, Leigh Rovarik could only wonder what was going on outside. When Sophie slid into the room, he signaled for her to be still.

A Sicilian bodyguard entered the building first and headed directly towards the inner offices. Next came Bishop Juan Carlos Ruiz, followed by two more bodyguards. Seconds later, Rovarik saw Archbishop Manuel Zagranski come in.

As he watched, he tried to decide how much time they would have to get out. He thought that the phony report Silas had faxed to Rome the night before obviously hadn't bought them much time. Ruiz and Zagranski must have *left Rome in the middle of the night to get here by now.*

"I want this place searched from top to bottom. Tear the damn place apart if you have to. What we are looking for is definitely in here somewhere." Zagranski issued the orders to no one in particular as they walked past the room where Leigh Rovarik and Sophie stood quietly.

"I will accept no more excuses. We have no time for mistakes." The archbishop glanced in the direction of the secretary's room.

"Our visitors, Father Hector. Would you like to say something to them?" Kneeling on the floor, Sister Marie looked up humbly as the priests walked by her.

Leigh was stunned by her request. His heart pounded as he waited for one of the priests to reply. If they saw him, it was all over.

"You imbecile," the young priest said. "Keep your mouth shut."

She bowed her head quickly, feeling stupid. She should not have spoken out.

Sophie edged closer to Father Rovarik and handed him his overcoat, feeling the same tension as he did. The evil force was much too close now. She could feel it in her blood. She waited anxiously for them to reach the end of the hallway. When they were out of sight, she knelt down beside the feebleminded, humiliated nun and put her arm around her. Feeling her tremble, she whispered a soft good-bye in her ear. "We don't want to be in the way, Sister. It looks like you have your hands full here. Thank you for everything. We'll see ourselves out."

As quickly and quietly as possible, they opened the door of Shelley House and walked out. Robert was anxiously awaiting them in a car outside the front gates. Once inside, Father Rovarik broke the silence. "Did you finish up with the banking, Robert?"

"Most of it, Father. Did you get what you came for?"

"I'm not sure. Did we, Sophie?"

"We got everything, Robert. Now can we please get the hell out of here?"

Father Rovarik fell silent again, thinking about what just happened. Someone was figuring things out too quickly, he thought. It was the only way the priests could have gotten here so fast. He decided it was very lucky that they had caught the early bus here this morning. An hour later and they would have been caught.

Wanting one last glimpse of the Opus Dei house, he pressed the button to lower the back window and looked out. Above him, a solitary man stood on a balcony over-looking the river and the Chelsea Embankment. Manuel Zagranski seemed to be staring right at him as their car pulled away and drove off towards the Albert Bridge.

TWENTY-SEVEN

**Monte Carlo
November 4**

*Robert and Sophie leave London
together with the secret*

A *Monaco sunset glittered brilliantly* on the blue green water as the ninety-foot yacht *Ezra Brooks* bobbed peacefully on its mooring in the harbor. Sophie was sitting alone on its bow, watching the surreal mix of cascading colors dance themselves up off the calm waters. The horizon seemed so close to her that she felt as if she could reach out and embrace it. The vision enveloped her like a transparent lover for only one brief second and then it vanished away.

With it went her amorous thoughts about Robert. Wishing them back, she began walking towards the stern of the boat. She could hear the chatter of those below as she passed by a porthole. Her name was mentioned several times.

Father Rovarik, Robert and Jamie were the ones immersed in the discussion below. "What about you and Sophie? Did you have any trouble getting here, Father?" Robert was the one asking the question.

"Not really. The Gypsies have a wonderful little underground. They can get you anywhere you want to go. And you?" His eyebrows rose slightly whenever he thought of the cleverness of his people.

"I *flew* into Nice and Jamie took a train down from Paris. We met in a bar there and drove over," Robert responded.

"Good," said Rovarik. "Now tell me more about the banks, Robert. What do you think was going on with the Venetian, Zagranski, Hernandez and the Opus Dei? And how did the church fit into all of it?" The mindful priest never wasted time.

"This is an involved story, Father, and I'm not sure I know everything that happened. But from what I've been able to gather so far, it went something like this." Robert stopped speaking abruptly. Muffled sounds came from the hatch. They all looked in that direction, alert for any intrusions.

"It's only me. The sun's going down and it's getting cold up there," Sophie said, lowering herself down the ladder steps.

Calmed, Robert picked up where he had left off. "The whole arrangement looks much different to me than I had initially thought it would be. When Sophie told me about the man called the Venetian who approached her and the cardinal with the London Boys' booty, I was a bit skeptical. Having played a part in the first transactions, I thought I knew everyone."

"When you say the London Boys, Robert, are you referring to Leonardo Roberto Calvi, Michele Sindona and Josemaria Ruiz-Mateos?" Father Rovarik asked.

"Yes, using Sophie's nickname. They were the three famous London Boys."

"Was Ruiz-Mateos related in any way to Bishop Juan Carlos Ruiz?"

"Yes, Father, a first cousin. That's why it was so easy to use the church. Family ties."

"Go on. I'll try not to interrupt you again." The priest leaned back.

"Well, everyone knew that a lot of money might still be missing from the London Boys' banks. And this fellow, the Venetian, was a new face in the crowd. So, I thought, let's see what's going on here. Maybe I didn't know everyone. Perhaps this guy really was a fourth London Boy. So I accepted the fact that somehow he ended up with the balance of what they stole and made a deal with Carmen Hernandez to get it all cleaned. Sophie was the go-between in the arrangement." Pausing briefly he gathered his thoughts and then went on.

"Carmen Hernandez appears to have felt he was blessed with a second windfall. And if everything had worked out like he anticipated, he would indeed have brought in a lot of fresh money for the Opus Dei. In doing so, he would have re-established his credibility with those in Rome who were getting a little tired of his extracurricular activities."

"Why do I think you're going to tell me something I don't want to hear?" Sophie said.

"Patience, dear. There have been some twists in all of this. Let me take it one step at a time."

The priest, too, wanted to press on. "You don't think it was a simple wash anymore, do you?"

"No, not at all. It's too sophisticated. But as I said, it's important that we put everything in its proper order. All in good time."

"I'm sorry. What's next?"

"Well, there's no doubt in my mind that the Venetian brought the stolen securities to Sophie and Cardinal Hernandez, along with the incriminating records. Once the money started going through the famous money-cleaning factory, he took out his portion and left. He gave you the copies of the records only after he got his money, right?"

Sophie nodded yes.

"We all know what happened next. After the securities were washed, Sophie stole the money and then sent it off to Andre Macheras. Hernandez, Zagranski and Ruiz all got screwed."

"And?" said Rovarik.

"Well, a couple of things don't make much sense to me. First, because of the magnitude of the money involved, I don't think the Venetian was acting alone. He had to have help. Possibly someone who had links to the Knights of Malta. Without a doubt, I believe he was involved with someone who knew a lot about the first washes. What works once will work again, or something like that. I also don't think any of them cared much about promoting the interests of the Opus Dei. They only needed their money cleaned. I strongly suspect that when Sophie called Andre, they looked at it as a wrinkle in their program—but also as an opportunity to better cover their asses."

Robert poured himself a glass of wine. "What else?"

"I strongly suspect that they never intended to let the money go to Rome. If Sophie hadn't rerouted the funds, I think they would have. But there are more pressing problems for us to deal with now than trying to figure out who was really running the show."

"What problems?" Father Rovarik asked.

Robert felt the tension in the cabin growing. "When I first began to collect our money in London, two documents mistakenly came in to me at once from one of the banks. They showed transfers which were being made from the same bank, at the same time our transfers were occurring, into some Caribbean accounts. At the time, I was so busy trying to recover our money that I didn't look closely at the wire transfer numbers."

"What did you find out?" Sophie was getting impatient hearing these things she had not been informed of earlier.

"Wouldn't you like to know how much money I got back first?" He paused waiting for her to ask him. When she didn't, he told her.

"I couldn't get it all back. But I did get a lot of it. I was able to recover just over $100 million. But guess what? As our wires were coming in, it looks like your friend Andre and his partners were taking out the same amounts themselves. The two documents I received show that the transfer numbers and the sums listed on our records correspond exactly to the ones sent into the Caribbean accounts. The ones made to us clearly list Sophie as being the recipient. Theirs have only numbers on them. It looks like they set it up so that if anyone asks, they can claim it all went to us, to you in particular, Sophie. Whoever is looking for their money will be after you. To use an old schoolyard expression, you're it." Mimicking the movements of the game, Robert tagged Sophie on the head gently.

Sophie said nothing. She was awestruck, not only at the amount of money Robert had recovered but also at the treachery of Andre and his friends.

Seeing Sophie's expression, Father Rovarik stopped him from going on. "Perhaps you're right, Robert, and they actually did do this, but we'll never know for sure. These international bankers are a greedy bunch and their power is a distortion of everything that is valuable. It's late, I'm tired, and we all need some rest. We'll talk more in the morning about the money and how to get Sophie out of this awful mess."

The priest blew out the kerosene lamp on the table and minutes later fell asleep thinking about something he had read in Saint Augustine's *City of God:* "When man lives according to human ways and not according to God's will, then he lives in falsehood."

TWENTY-EIGHT

November 5

The True History of Jesus Christ is told

Sophie was the first one up the next morning, joined by Robert as soon as the coffee had perked. "Did you sleep well?" Robert asked with a yawn, handing her his cup to fill.

"Give me a break. Did you? Do you think we'll ever get out of this?"

"I think I've come up with a way, Sophie. Listen up."

Twenty minutes later they were still discussing his plan, when they were disturbed.

"Good morning," Father Rovarik said, emerging from the fore cabin. Jamie was straggling in after him. "Are we interrupting anything?"

"Nothing that can't wait." Robert answered.

"Good. Then let's talk about our next little excursion. The one we're going to make to Rome."

"Why Rome?" Sophie was curious.

"Let's just say we're going to bring in some things that *they aren't expecting.*"

Not having to be asked, they all helped open the drop-table for breakfast. Jamie went to the cupboards and refrigerator and emerged with a box of cereal and a carton of milk.

"What things?" Sophie needed some answers.

"Putting the money issues aside for the time being, do any of you know anything about the cloth I have?"

They all shook their heads no.

"Then it's time I tell you something about it. It's a relatively simple story in contrast to the complicated world of international banking and intrigue." Pushing aside his bowl, he began to tell them about the cloth.

"As we know, there were a number of significant periods in *our Lord's life*. The first twelve and the last three years, we know a lot about. *But the middle years are a mystery*. It is thought that at some point in his life, Christ traveled widely. Many scholars believe that during these missing years he went with nomadic caravans to the areas of Persia, Afghanistan, Tibet and Kashmir. If this *is true*, He most likely traveled with the Gypsies to Tibetan and Kashmiri monasteries. Legend has it that He did. Legend also has it that after He died, *many of His followers returned to these same holy places*.

Feeling moved just talking about these things; the priest took a few seconds to catch his breath. "It is thought that Christ gave the cloth that I have to the apostle Paul just before the Crucifixion. Somehow it found its way up to one of the monasteries and has been kept there for centuries. Years ago, *my sister* went looking for it. She found it there and brought it down to Rome. After passing through Escriva's fingers there, it came to me. It is also thought that a second holy cloth exists. This one still has not been located. According to prophecy, a day will come when the two pieces of cloth will be brought to the actual place of Christ's death and placed over the sacred rock at the altar of Golgotha in the Church of the Holy Sepulcher. At that time, something fabulous will happen."

He paused again. "But the legend also says that this can only happen when the religious leaders of the world pray together to move the cloths there. Those who do will be embraced by the Savior when He comes to judge us. The others will not be saved."

Father Rovarik looked at each of the three before continuing. "Being realistic, this unification is not likely to happen soon. So the best we can do is to alert the pope about the possibilities. Our cloth is his call-to-arms to help make that moment come. We are going to Rome to entice him with the fact that we have it."

"Let's discuss the money," Robert said abruptly. He was a lot less interested in the history of a 2,000-year-old relic than he was in money.

"The funds we recovered should be turned around, Father," Sophie intervened.

"What does this mean, 'turned around?'" Father Rovarik was surprised at their lack of interest in the holy relic and wasn't sure what they meant.

"It's what we were talking about when you came in. We want to set up a church fund. It will be called the Galilee Fund and will be used to help the victims of the bank frauds who went broke because of what the London Boys and the church did."

"It's a way of getting Sophie out of this, Father. If we give the money to the church, the bad guys will go after the Opus Dei." Robert smiled thinking about what a novel idea it was.

"Interesting." Father Rovarik was amused. "How difficult is this to do?"

"Setting up a fund is easy, Father. Jamie can shuttle back to London, do what I tell him to do, fax me the papers at our hotel in Rome and then catch up with us later," Robert offered.

"Who would manage the fund and give out the money?" Jamie asked.

Understanding the plan, Father Rovarik answered him. "This will be another little surprise we'll bring in with us. They did the damage; they can pay the consequences. We'll ask the boys at the Vatican to administer the refunds."

"But that would be an open admission of guilt on their part." Jamie wasn't sure those in Rome would accept these terms.

"Precisely. But if they don't, the Gypsies will get to keep their cardinal. I wonder how he's enjoying desert life." The priest smiled.

"If we all agree, then I think it's time to prepare ourselves for Rome, children. You arrange for the fund and there are a number of people I have to contact to help us when we get there. We should all be ready for Sunday Mass at Saint Peter's. If we're good boys and girls, perhaps they won't charge us admission to get up into the Sistine Chapel to see Michelangelo's paintings."

TWENTY-NINE

Rome
November 8

The Secretary to the Pope is exposed
for his treacherous plot at

— Saint Peters Basilica —

Father Rovarik, Sophie and Robert paid little attention to the tourists or the magnificent white obelisk in the center of St. Peter's Square which marked the exact spot where Christ's favorite apostle was crucified upside down in Nero's circus. They were in a hurry. Their audience with Pope John Paul II was in 20 minutes. The one he didn't know about. Together they climbed the stone steps leading up to the basilica.

Inside, the church was packed full. But unlike the bustle of the courtyard outside, it was quiet. Father Rovarik took them past the Peter's Pence collection coffers to an empty space near the last row of wooden chairs, where they would not be in the way.

The first thing Sophie noticed was the unbelievable size of the main section of the church. Father Rovarik had told her on the way over that 100,000 people could worship here at one time. He wasn't exaggerating. The cathedral was immense and the art was magnificent. Murals by the great masters covered the walls and ceilings. Priceless mosaics and unbelievable gold articles adorned every side altar. Bronze and marble statues and monuments were everywhere. The church was a glorious museum. Above, in one of the choir lofts, a woman accompanied by a pipe organ was singing "And the Glory of the Lord" from Handel's *Messiah*. It was serene.

Standing beside Sophie, Father Rovarik was scanning the aisles looking for his brother, who was supposed to meet them at the entrance.

"I thought you said he'd be waiting for us," Robert whispered as they began to weave their way through the throngs of parishioners who had come for the ailing pope's service.

"He's in here somewhere. Don't worry," Father Rovarik answered softly. As soon as the words left his lips, he saw his brother coming towards him from one of the penitentiaries. The huge Gypsy extended his long arms to his older brother and gave him a strong hug. A small group of black-robed priests and nuns with him encircled Father Rovarik. Then one of the younger priests took Leigh by the arm and led them all to a side altar where about 300 more clergymen and women waited.

Forming a procession, they walked toward the front altar where the pope was celebrating Mass. As the holy alliance reached the main aisle, the music stopped. After a split second of silence, they all began to pray out loud. Once they did, every person in the first five rows lit a round white candle and turned to wait for the assembly to reach the front of the cathedral.

Poised to consecrate the sacred host, the pontiff looked up in surprise. He whispered a query to one of the cardinals standing beside him who, knowing no more than he left the altar to confer with others in crimson hats and several bishops. One of them was Archbishop Manuel Zagranski.

The procession continued to advance itself down the main aisle. Leigh Rovarik was at its head with Sophie and Robert on either side of him. Sophie carried a black nylon pack containing a duplicate set of the Venetian's *records* and *copies of the tapes* she had made of the meetings between the Venetian, Carmen and herself. Robert carried the *faxed copies* of the deposit receipts for the new Galilee Fund.

When they reached the altar the pope came around to greet them. Seeing Father Rovarik, he smiled and extended his right hand to him. The humble old priest knelt down and tenderly kissed the pope's ring. Then he stood back up and told Sophie and Robert to place their offerings on the altar.

"What is all this, my son?" The pope looked at him lovingly.

Tears flowed from the priest's eyes as he looked sadly to his beloved pope. Pausing briefly to return the same type of gaze Zagranski had given him in London, he collected himself and said, in a voice that could be heard throughout the cathedral, "Papa. We must talk. We have bad troubles. Christ has been betrayed."

THIRTY

Six Hours Later

The brotherhood leader is revealed as being Two-Faced

The Awful Dream (Nightmare) is used as bookends — In both the beginning and the end of the story

The three were still cooling down from the powerful emotional experience in the basilica and the ensuing discussion that took place in the private offices of the pope. They were sitting at a sidewalk cafe near the train station discussing everything.

"What do you think he's going to do, Father?" Sophie was really asking if things were getting any closer to being over for her.

"I'm hoping he'll have the good sense to appoint an impartial church commission to investigate the larcenies. There is no doubt in my mind that he will name someone to administer the refunds." Father Rovarik knew that their public display hadn't left the pope much choice.

"What about Zagranski?" Robert was looking for his own information.

"I think he will have his problems, as will Carmen Hernandez, Juan Carlos Ruiz and everyone else who was involved in this unholy business. These troubled souls will not leave this life unpunished."

"What about us?" Robert asked.

"Speaking for myself, I'm going back to Galilee. My work there is unfinished. What are you going to do, Sophie?"

"I haven't had much time to think about it, Father. I wasn't sure I would ever get out of this." She glanced at Robert, hoping he would say something about their future together.

The old priest looked compassionately at her, knowing her desire to settle down, thinking how sad it is when love tries to compete with greed and how sometimes even miracles don't change what is in a person's heart.

"I want to hear more about the cloths," Robert said, quick to change the subject.

Rovarik held up two fingers and signaled the waiter to bring another round of coffees.

"The cloths are marvelous memories, Robert."
"What do you mean?" Sophie asked.

"Have either of you ever been to Bethlehem?"
"No."

"It's a very interesting place. The town where Christ was born is much different from the portrayals we see or the descriptions we read. Do you have any idea what the actual birthplace of Jesus looks like"?

"No."

"Its presentation as an outdoor stable is extremely misleading. The stable was actually underground. Christ's manger was in a cave."

The waiter arrived with their espressos. Once he left, the priest went on. "To get to the manger, you first go through a hole cut into the remains of a wall in a deserted old church. Then you walk down a path to the cave opening. You climb through the mouth of the cave and then descend a few steep steps to the place where the stalls were when Christ was born. The one on the left is where the manger was. Anyone who has ever visited it knows that it is cut out of solid rock. It is a trough."

"What does a trough have to do with memories?" Robert impatiently rephrased his question.

"Quite a bit, but you'll have to humor me a little, Robert. First, close your eyes and free your minds. Let me borrow your senses for a few moments."

They did as he asked and closed their eyes.

"Good. Now, imagine that it is a time long ago. You are in this place I have described, this hole in the ground, in a cave. It is a cold, frigid night. The wind is blowing wildly at the opening. A fire has been lit, but there is little heat. Except for reflections and shadows, it is dark. There is a baby and three adults there, a man and two women. Although you can't see well, you can hear. There are noises outside, terrible noises, the growling of packs of wild dogs trying to get in.

But something is stopping them. Hours go by. The growling continues all night. Finally, the morning light brings peace. The dogs are gone. When you look to the cave opening, you see two cloths hanging like curtains, one on each side. These cloths are what shielded the Christ child from the terrors outside during his first night on earth."

Opening their eyes Sophie and Robert began to understand the significance of the relics. They were Christ's first memories.

"You have seen the powers of the cloths. Can you imagine their worth? If the Opus Dei possessed either of them, there would be no doubt that Escriva would be canonized. Performing miracles after one's death is credible criteria. And Manuel Zagranski's own aspirations would also be realized. *In all likelihood he would be **the next pope**.*"

Father Rovarik folded his hands in his lap, satisfied that he had told them enough about the holy cloths. His movement was a signal that the discussion about them was ended.

"So my children. We must part ways. But before I leave you, I wonder if you would help me tie up a few loose ends I have with this money business." The priest was looking directly at Robert.

"What do you want to know?" Robert asked, concerned by the priest's apparent resolve.

"Well, Robert. I can accept most of your explanations concerning the time frames and movements of the money through the banks. But some things are still unclear to me."

"What?"

"I agree with your assessment that the Venetian was sent by someone to see Sophie and Carmen Hernandez. I understand that a deal was made to bring in the residual stolen securities he had, and that Sophie turned the whole thing upside down by her actions."

He paused to allow them to concentrate on what he was saying. "I'm confused, though. When Sophie began to steal the money, why didn't someone stop her?"

"Because by the time they knew what was going on, the wash was over. The money was coming back in to us and then going out again. One transaction produced a whole series of other transactions," Sophie answered him.

"Who arranged the banking?"

Again it was Sophie who responded. "I managed it once the money got into the foundation's accounts. Carmen set up the wash processes."

"Don't you think that if he was really in charge he would have known when things were going awry?" The priest looked at her, surprised that she hadn't thought about this.

Robert broke in. "It all happened too fast. The money flows were set up like Sophie said they were. She just changed the flow route, that's all. She redirected everything over to Andre's banks."

The priest encouraged Robert to continue. He did. "Andre and his were trying to protect the interests of the Knights of Malta. They were using the Opus Dei priests to process the dirty money," he said, repeating what he had told them earlier on the yacht in Monte Carlo.

"I think you are partly correct, Robert. The Venetian was just a front man. But I just don't think it was the Knights of Malta who sent him in." Again he paused, respecting the gravity of the conversation. "I think it was someone who the Opus Dei priests trusted. A person who participated in the first deals with the London Boys, someone who somehow managed to acquire the balance of their securities and was manipulating Carmen Hernandez. This person apparently decided it was a good time to break free of them. I would guess that Sophie's state of mind, her position at the foundation and her relationship with Carmen Hernandez were factors in his decision."

The priest stopped again, then continued. "I'm not doubting that things happened the way you told us they did, Sophie. But someone else was in control of this game, not Carmen Hernandez. And this person was playing on both sides of the fence. When you changed the rules, so did he. He used the situation you created to his financial advantage. He allowed you to reroute the funds because he knew he'd be able to use his influence over the priests and you to get at the money."

"But the money is in the Galilee Fund now. The pope and the church are the only ones who have access to it. That's how we got Sophie out of this mess," Robert said.

The priest did not accept the fact that Sophie was out of danger. "I became suspicious when Manuel Zagranski showed up so fast in London. The only way he could have known about us being at Shelley House was for someone who participated in our discussions the previous night to have told him that we were there. It had to be someone who wasn't interested in the cloth, just the money. I believe that this someone was hoping that the priests would take us out of the picture."

"What purpose would that have served?" Robert asked.

"With Sophie and me out of the way, anyone looking for their money would go after the Opus Dei priests."

"It was most likely Willoughby who called them." Sophie offered her own evaluation of what happened.

"Not likely. I don't think he was in a frame of mind to call anyone. The morning after he sent them our fax, he was picked up walking aimlessly through the streets of London blabbering something about just seeing Jesus Christ. He's still in the psychiatric unit of a London hospital."

"But neither of you were ever in danger. You're sitting right here and you both look fine to me, and they can't get anything back from the church." Robert said.

"I think you're right about some things, Robert. Andre and his Knights probably did keep a lot of Sophie's money. There was no reason for them not to. And it's true that the church has some of what was thrown back, in order, I suspect, to lead the Sicilians away. But I think that a very large amount of what was recovered never ended up in the Galilee Fund. You see, the person I am speaking of was not satisfied with the payments he received for the stolen securities he sold to the priests. When chance presented itself, he went after more money. When the game got complicated, he played on. When someone interfered, he deceived or got rid of them. After the money came in, he grabbed what he could and then threw some crumbs back to create a little confusion. Now he is trying to lead everyone off in different directions, hoping they won't find him out." He looked severely at Robert.

"Robert. You did all of this?" Sophie suddenly felt physically ill.

The old priest didn't let up. "Playing by your rules, we got as much of the money back as we could. The rest we'll see about later. By the way, Robert, I have a strong suspicion that more than a few people will make this person pay dearly for his activities."

"Sophie," the priest said, "do you remember telling me on the way over from France about *your dreams? Where the dragon is scratching and crawling after you as you're trying to cross over the Bridge of Dread*?"

"Yes," Sophie murmured. She really didn't want to hear any more.

"Meet your demon, Sophie. For all practical purposes, the *Four...th London Boy*."

Robert scowled and put his arm around Sophie. He whispered a few soft, mocking words to her, but she knew that the priest would never lie to her. "How could you do this, Robert? How could you be so damn heartless?"

"You shouldn't have fucked the cardinal, Sophie." Remembering the rejection he had felt when she'd had the affair with Hernandez, Robert said what he'd been thinking for a long time.

Leigh Rovarik looked at Sophie, feeling fatherly again. He knew this experience was going to make her strong and that she was almost across her dreaded bridge. But he also saw her pain. He decided that he could help ease it by removing her from its cause. "I'm going to the airport, Sophie. Why don't you hitch a ride with me? There's nothing left for you here. What's here is evil, corrupted. There's a dying in Canada who has been asking for you. Perhaps it's time to pay her a visit."

They rose from the table and quietly distanced themselves from the miserably obsessed chameleon of a man who no one really knew. The only thing Sophie could think about as they crossed the street to the taxi stand was when would her magical horse Buddy come and make this nightmare end?

Minutes after they left, a limousine pulled up to the curb. Robert stood up, paid the check and got into the car. Neither he nor Jamie noticed the dark green *Fiat* behind them. Jamie was too busy talking about how much money they had made. Robert didn't respond to his excitement. There was no need to. He stared blankly out the windshield, knowing they weren't going far. Leigh Rovarik knew too much and he wasn't going to let them get away.

THIRTY-ONE

Israel
May 6, 1997

One half of the puzzle appears

The jet engines roared as the plane landed at the Tel Aviv airport in Israel. Listening to them, Father Sean O'Toole grieved at the news of the trials taking place back in Italy and the commission's findings concerning the church's involvement in the filthy banking business of the last twenty years. It made him ill to think that plea bargains had been offered to Robert Hathaway and Jamie Cole in exchange for their cooperation.

But, he told himself, things were getting straightened out, and if situations like these weren't dealt with openly, they would happen again. Glancing at the newspaper headlines, he reiterated his vow to do everything in his power to help right the wrongs that had been perpetrated in the name of God by members of his church.

He began to prepare himself inwardly for what promised to be a very difficult time. He was glad to be in the Holy Land but wished the circumstances surrounding his visit were different.

Collecting his belongings he started down the aisle, praying silently to the Blessed Virgin Mary for her continued guidance and support.

The young priest understood that killings and other acts of violence were a hideous, but real part of life. It was one of these tragedies that had brought him here. Leigh Rovarik had asked him to make this journey if anything happened to him or the relic. Something had. Wire service accounts reported that the priest had been murdered by members of a militant fundamentalist group who had been looking for a valuable relic. Sean knew differently. It had been the Opus Dei who had come after him.

As he emerged from the aircraft and felt the blistering hot sun shining down upon him, he hoped that *the relic* was still where Leigh Rovarik had told him it would be, when they had walked together in the procession on that sacred day not too long ago in Saint Peter's. The Irish priest had come here to recover it and to pay his last respects to a martyr, the Gypsy priest from Galilee.

EPILOGUE

**The Himalayas
June 22, 1997**

*An old Woman's 'ashes' are underground,
in a poorly lit cavern, in a 'golden urn'*

The second half of the puzzle appears

*Two sacred objects joined together are
— One*

Listening to the pounding avalanches outside the monastery, two monks removed *the second holy cloth* from beneath *the golden urn* that held the revered Gypsy *woman's ashes*. They folded it, bowed respectfully to the Buddha there and left the room. A long, *dimly lit hallway* led them down to a series of *underground caves*. As they walked, the younger monk asked his companion, "When do you think they will be ready for this cloth?" The older monk didn't really know the answer to the question. "Some now, some never," he said, "but they will all experience its power soon. We are bringing this cloth down to the church in Jerusalem. He is coming back, with their help or without it." As they padded their way towards *the deep caverns*, they chanted only one word: "Soon."

The End

Printed in Great Britain
by Amazon